Survival . . . Zero!

"Hi, Pat. I got a stiff for you."

Softly, Pat muttered, "Damn, Mike . . ."

"Hell," I told him, "I didn't do it."

"Okay, give me the details."

I gave him the address on West Forty-sixth, Lippy's full name and told him the rest could wait. I didn't want the guy behind me getting an earful and Pat got the message. He told me a squad car was on the way and he'd be right behind it. I hung up and lit a butt.

It was an election year and all the new brooms were waiting to sweep clean. The old ones were looking to sweep cleaner. It was another murder now, a nice, messy, newspaper-type murder and both sides would love to make me a target. I'd been in everybody's hair just too damn long, I guess.

MICKEY SPILLANE

Survival . . . Zero!

Mandarin

A Mandarin Paperback

SURVIVAL . . . ZERO!

First published by E.P. Dutton & Company Inc.
First published in Great Britain 1970
by Transworld Publishers Ltd
This edition published 1990
by Mandarin Paperbacks
Michelin House, 81 Fulham Road, London SW3 6RB

Mandarin is an imprint of the Octopus Publishing Group

Copyright © 1970 by Mickey Spillane

A CIP catalogue record for this book
is available from the British Library
ISBN 0 7493 0274 7

Printed in Great Britain
by Cox & Wyman Ltd, Reading

To Jack and Peggy McKenna
With thanks for the many happy returns

Survival . . . Zero!

CHAPTER 1

They had left him for dead in the middle of a pool of blood in his own bedroom, his belly slit open like gaping barn doors, the hilt of the knife wedged against his sternum. But the only trouble was that he had stayed alive somehow, his life pumping out, managing to knock the telephone off the little table and dial me. Now he was looking up at me with seconds left and all he could do was force out the words, "Mike . . . there wasn't no reason."

I didn't try to fake him out. He knew what was happening. I said, "Who, Lippy?"

His lips fought to frame the sentence. "Nobody I . . . not the kind. . . .No reason, Mike. No reason."

And then Lippy Sullivan died painfully but quickly.

I went out in the hallway of the shabby brownstone rooming house and walked up to the front apartment that had SUPER scrawled across the top panels in faded white paint and gave it a rap with the toe of my shoe. Inside, somebody swore hoarsely and a chair scraped across bare wood. Two locks and a bolt rasped in their sockets and the door cracked open on a safety chain.

The fat-faced guy with the beery breath squinted up at me in the light from behind him, then his eyes narrowed, not liking what he saw. "Yeah?"

"You got a phone, buddy?"

"What if I do?"

"You can let me use it."

"Drop dead." He started to close the door, but I already had my foot in the crack.

I said, "Open up."

For a second his jowls seemed to sag, then he got his beer courage back up again. "You a cop? Let's see your badge."

"I'll show you more than a badge in a minute."

This time he didn't try smart-mouthing me. I let him close the door, slide the chain off, then pushed in past

9

him. The room was a home-grown garbage collection, but I found the phone behind a pile of empty six-pack cartons, dialed my number and a solid Brooklyn voice said, "Homicide South, Sergeant Woods."

"Captain Chambers in? This is Mike Hammer."

Behind me a beer can popped open and the fat guy slid onto a chair.

When the phone was picked up I said, "Hi, Pat. I got a stiff for you."

Softly, Pat muttered, "Damn, Mike . . ."

"Hell," I told him, "I didn't do it."

"Okay, give me the details."

I gave him the address on West Forty-sixth, Lippy's full name and told him the rest could wait. I didn't want the guy behind me getting an earful and Pat got the message. He told me a squad car was on the way and he'd be right behind it. I hung up and lit a butt.

It was an election year and all the new brooms were waiting to sweep clean. The old ones were looking to sweep cleaner. It was another murder now, a nice, messy, newspaper-type murder and both sides would love to make me a target. I'd been in everybody's hair just too damn long, I guess.

When I turned around the fat guy was sweating. The empty beer can had joined the others on the table beside him.

"Who's . . . the stiff?"

"A tenant named Lippy Sullivan."

"Who'd want to kill him?"

I shoved my hat back and walked over to where he was sitting and let him look at the funny grin I knew I was wearing. "He have anybody in with him tonight?"

"Listen, Mister . . ."

"Just answer me."

"I didn't hear nothin'."

"How long you been here?" I said.

"All night. I been sitting here all night and I didn't hear nothin'."

I let the grin go a little bigger and the grin wasn't pretty at all. "You better be right," I told him. "Now sit here some more and think about things and maybe something might come back to you."

He gave me a jerky nod, reached for another beer and watched me leave. I went back to Lippy's room, nudged the door open and stepped inside again. Somebody was going to give me hell for not calling an ambulance, but I

10

had seen too many dead men to be bothered taking a call away from somebody who might really need it.

Death was having a peculiar effect on the body. In just a few minutes it had released the premature aging and all the worry had relaxed from his face. I said softly, "Adios, Lippy," then took a good look at the room. Not that there was much to see. There were hundreds more just like it in the neighborhood, cheap one-room fleabags with a bed, some assorted pieces of furniture and a two-burner gas range on top of a secondhand dresser in one corner. The only thing that looked new was an inexpensive daybed against the far wall and from the way the mattress sagged on the brass four-poster I could see why he'd needed it.

I used a handkerchief, pulled out the dresser drawers, and fingered through the odds and ends that made up Lippy's wardrobe. Nothing was neat or orderly, but that was Lippy, all right. Just another guy alone who didn't give a damn about having ironed socks and shorts. The closet held a single wrinkled suit, some work clothes carelessly tossed onto hooks, two pairs of worn shoes and an old Army raincoat. I patted the pockets down. One pair of pants held three singles and a lunch ticket. There was nothing else.

Outside I heard the whine of a siren coming closer, then cut out when the squad car reached the building. I went over and elbowed the door open. Two uniformed cops came in properly geared for action. I said, "Over here." Another car pulled up and I heard a door slam. Pat hadn't wasted any time.

The lab technicians had dusted, photographed and taken the body away. All that was left of Lippy was a chalked outline on the floor beside the sticky damp sawdust that had soaked up his blood. I walked over and sat on the couch and waited until Pat slumped wearily into a chair that looked as tired as he was.

Finally Pat said, "You ready now, Mike?"

I nodded.

"Want me to take notes?" Pat asked.

"You'll get the report in the morning. Let's make it real official."

"We'd better. I know people who'd like to burn your ass for anything at all. They might even make it on this one. So let's hear the story. Once more, from the top."

"Lippy . . . Lipton Sullivan," I said. "We went to school together. He dropped out at the ninth grade and we met

11

up again in the Army for a while. No record I know of. Just a hard-luck character who couldn't make it in this world. Two years ago I got him a job checking out groceries in a wholesale warehouse."

"See him often?"

"Only once since then. We had a couple of drinks together. He insisted on buying. Nice guy, but a born loser."

Pat rubbed his hand across his eyes before looking up. "Heavy drinker?"

"Nope. He rarely touched the stuff."

"Broads?"

"I told you he was a loser. Besides, he never was a big one for women. They seemed to be mutually unattractive to one another."

This time Pat waited a long time before he spoke. "I don't like it, Mike."

"I can't blame you."

"No ... I don't mean that."

"So?"

"You're involved, old buddy. I know what happens when you get involved. Right now you sit there and play it cool, but you know you're damn well involved ..."

"Nuts," I said. "He was a guy I knew, that's all."

"He didn't call the cops, Mike. He called you. When was the last time he did that?"

"When I got him that job. He thanked me."

"That was two years ago, you said. You changed your number since then."

I grinned at him and reached for a cigarette. "You're still pretty sharp, kid," I told him. "No phone directory here, no memos in the papers on him so he must have memorized my new number."

"Something like that."

"Maybe he wanted to thank me again."

"Can it."

"So I'm his only famous friend." I fired up the butt and blew a stream of gray smoke toward the ceiling.

"Let's take the other reason why I don't like it."

"Go ahead."

"For a nothing guy like him it's too nasty a kill. Now suppose we see how smart you still are, friend."

I glanced over at the discolored sawdust and felt my mouth turn sour. "One of three things. A psycho kill, a revenge kill or a torture kill. He could have stayed alive a long time with his belly slit open before somebody pounded the knife into his chest."

"Which one, Mike?" Pat's voice had a curious edge to it.

My own voice sounded strange. "I don't know yet."

"Yet?"

"Why don't you handle it your own way?" I said.

"I'd love to, but I got that funny feeling again, Mike. Sometimes I can smell the way you think."

"Not this time."

"Okay, I'll buy it for now. See you in the morning?"

"Roger, kiddo."

The Blue Ribbon Restaurant on West Forty-fourth had closed an hour ago, but George and his wife were keeping Velda company in a corner booth over endless pots of coffee, and when I came in she gave me one of those "You did it again" looks and propped her chin on her hands, patiently waiting for an explanation. I sat down next to her, brushed my lips across that beautiful auburn pageboy roll of hair that curled around her shoulders and patted her thigh gently. "Sorry, honey," I said.

George shook his head in mock wonder and poured my coffee. "How you can stand up somebody like your girl here gets me, Mike. Now you take a Greek like me . . ."

His wife threw the hooks right into him. "To see *my* husband, I have to work the cash register. He loves this place more than he does me."

"Business is business," I reminded her.

Velda let her hand fall on top of mine and the warmth of her skin was like a gentle massage. "What happened, Mike?"

"Lippy Sullivan got himself sliced to death."

"*Lippy?*"

"Don't ask me why. That cat never did anything to get himself a smack in the eye. Somebody just got to him and took him apart. It could have been for any reason. Hell, in that neighborhood, you can get knocked off for a dime. Look at that wino last week . . . murder for a half bottle of muscatel. Two days before and a block away some old dame gets mugged and killed for a three-dollar take. Great. Fun City at its best. If the pollution doesn't get you, the traffic will. If you live through those two you're fair game for the street hunters. So stay under the lights, kids, and carry a roll of quarters in your fist. The damn liberals haven't outlawed money as a deadly weapon yet."

Velda's fingers squeezed around mine. "Did they find anything?"

"What the hell would Lippy have? A few bucks in his

13

pocket, an almost punched-out lunch ticket, and some old clothes. But the lab'll come up with something. Any nut who killed like that wouldn't be careful about keeping it clean. It's just a stupid murder that happened to a nice guy."

"Nobody heard anything?" Velda asked me.

"The way he got sliced he wasn't about to yell or anything else. Anybody could have walked in there, knocked on his door, got in and laid a blade on him. The front door was open, the super had his TV going and a belly full of beer and if anybody on the block saw anything they haven't said so this far."

"Mike . . . you said he had a few dollars . . ."

"Stuffed into his watch pocket," I interrupted. "They don't even make pants with them any more."

"There has to be a reason for murder, Mike."

"Not always," I told her. "Not any more. It's getting to be a way of life."

We finished our coffee, said so long to George and his wife and grabbed a cab on the corner of Sixth Avenue. It was a corner I couldn't remember any longer. All the old places were gone and architectural hangovers towered into the night air, the windows like dimly lit dead eyes watching the city gasping harder for breath every day.

New York was going to hell with itself. A monumental tombstone to commercialism.

When we reached Velda's apartment she looked at me expectantly. "Nightcap?"

"Can I pass this time?"

"You're rough on a woman's ego. I had something special to show you."

"I'd be lacking appreciation tonight, kitten."

Her gentle smile told me all I needed to know. She had been around me too long not to recognize the signs. "You have to do it, Mike."

"Just to make sure. The damn thing bugs me."

"I understand. I'll see you at the office tomorrow." She leaned over, tasted my mouth with hers and brushed her fingers down my cheek. I said good night, watched her go into the building and told the driver to take me home.

The killing of Lippy Sullivan was only a one-column squib in the morning papers, the body being reported as having been discovered by a friend. Political news, a suspected gangland rubout of a prominent hood and the latest antics of a jet set divorce trial made Lippy the nonentity in death that he was in life.

14

My official statement had been taken down by a bored steno, signed, and Pat and I sat back to enjoy the cardboard-container tasting coffee. Ever since I had come in he had been giving me a funny, wary-eyed look and I was waiting for him to spit out what was on his mind. He took his own sweet time about it, swinging around in his swivel chair and making small talk.

Finally Pat said, "We were lucky on this one, buddy."

"How?"

"Your name didn't bring the grand explosion I thought it would."

I shrugged and took a sip of the coffee. It was bitter. "Maybe the old days are gone."

"Not with this bunch in office. When Schneider got knocked off last night it gave them something bigger to play with."

I put the empty container on his desk and sat back. "Quit playing games, Pat," I said.

He stopped swinging in the chair and gave me another of those looks again. "I got the lab report. A practically untraceable knife, no prints on the weapon at all ... nothing. The only prints on the doorknob were yours, so the killer apparently used gloves. Six other sets of prints were picked up in the room ... Lippy's, the super's, two guys from the furniture store on Eighth Avenue who moved in a couch for him and two unidentified. The super had the idea that Lippy was friendly with a guy upstairs who used to have a beer with him now and then. He moved out a week ago. No forwarding address."

"And the other set?"

"We're running them through R and I now. If we don't have anything, Washington may come up with a lead."

"You're sure going to a lot of trouble," I said.

"Murders are murders. We're not concerned with a pedigree."

"This is old Mike you're jazzing now, friend. You're making like it was a prime project."

Pat waited a minute, his face tight, then: "You holding back, Mike?"

"For Pete's sake, what the hell kind of a deal is this? So I knew the guy. We weren't roommates. You get a lousy kill in your lap and right away you got me slanted for working an angle. Come off it."

"Okay, relax. But don't say I haven't got just cause, kid. Knowing a guy's enough to get you kicking around and that's just what I don't want."

"Balls."

15

"All right," he told me, "we checked Lippy out ... his employers gave him a clean bill. He worked hard at a low-paying job, never any absenteeism, he was a friendly, well-liked guy ... no previous history of trouble, didn't drink, gamble, and he paid his bills. He got himself killed, but he had memorized your number beforehand."

Pat stopped for a second and I said, "Go on."

"The lab came up with something else. There were traces of tape adhesive around his mouth. Nobody heard him yell because he didn't. Your friend Lippy was gagged, tortured and finally stabbed to death. The way we reconstructed it was that the killer simply walked in off the street, knocked on the door, was admitted, knocked Lippy out, searched the place and when he didn't find what he was after, took him apart with a knife."

I looked at Pat curiously and said, "Nice, real nice. Why don't you fill in the holes? I was there too."

Pat nodded and sat back again, still watching me. "There was a contusion behind Lippy's ear that apparently came from a padded billy. Certain articles were out of position indicating a search of the premises. Or did you poke around?"

"A little," I admitted. "I didn't disturb anything."

"This was a search. Expert, but noticeable."

"For what?"

"That's what I'd like to know." I got another one of those long searching looks again. "He was your friend, Mike. What aren't you telling me?"

"Man, you're a hard one to convince."

"Let the details filter upstairs to one of those new bright boys in the D.A.'s office and they'll be even harder to convince. Right now there's not much noise because Lippy wasn't much of a guy, but somebody's going to read these reports, and somebody's going to start making waves. And, friend, they'll break right over your head."

"Once more around the track, Pat," I said. "You know everything I know. Just hope those prints show something. If I can think of anything you'll get it fast and in triplicate. Who's assigned to the case?"

"Jenkins and Wiley. They've been drawing all blanks too. Nobody saw or heard anything. Wiley's been using an informer we have on the block and the guy says the talk is square. The oddballs are coming and going in that neighborhood all the time and nobody pays any attention to them. They might come up with a lead, but the longer it takes the slimmer the chances are."

"Sorry about that."

Pat grunted and gave me a relieved grin. "Okay, pal. I don't like to lay it on either. I guess there can be one kill in the city that doesn't have to have you involved in it."

I stood up and put on my hat. "Hell," I said, "I'm too old for that crap any more anyway."

He gave me another of those unintelligible grunts and nodded thoughtfully. "Yeah, *sure* you are," he said.

The cabbie wanted to edge out of the heavy traffic so he cut over to Eighth Avenue going north and stayed in the fire lane, making the lights at a leisurely pace. I cranked the window down and let the thick air of the city slap at the side of my face, heavy with smells from the sidewalk markets, laced with the acrid tang of exhaust fumes that belched out of laboring trucks and buses. The voice of the city kept up its incessant growl, like a dog who didn't know whom to pick on and settled on everybody in general. *Most people out there never even heard the voice*, I thought. *Even the smells were the natural condition of things. Someday I was going to get the hell out of here. I was glad I had nothing to do about Lippy. So he was a guy I knew. I knew lots of guys. Some were alive. Some were dead.*

Then we were almost at Forty-sixth Street and I wondered who the hell I thought I was fooling and told the driver to pull over and let me out. I handed him a couple of singles, slammed the door, watched him pull away and crossed the street over to where Lippy Sullivan had died such a messy death. All I could say to myself was, *"Damn!"*

CHAPTER 2

The fat little super who smelled of sweat and beer didn't give me any lip this time. It wasn't because of the first time or because he had seen me there in the midst of the homicide squad with a gold shield cop my buddy. It was because I was the same kind of New York he was, only from a direction he was afraid of. There was nothing he could put his finger on; a squawk wouldn't bother me and could hurt him, and if he didn't play it nice and easy he could play it hard and get himself squeezed.

So he played it right and whined how he had told everything he knew which wasn't anything at all and let me into Lippy's room with his passkey, idly complaining about how he had to clean up the mess that had been left around before the flies got into it and the stink got worse than it was. Nobody paid him extra and the damn nosy cops wouldn't let him rent the room out until the investigation was over and he was losing a commission.

I shoved him out of the room, slammed the door in his face and flipped the overhead light on with my elbow. The stain was still there on the floor, but the sawdust was gone and so was the chalked outline of Lippy's body. And so was Lippy's new couch. I had seen it in the super's apartment when he had opened the door for me.

There wasn't anything special to look for. The cops had done all that. What I wanted was to know Lippy just a little bit better. I could remember a skinny little kid with a banana stalk in a street fight, swinging it out against the Peterstown bunch, then the soda bottle collection to pay for the six stitches the doctor over Delaney's Drugstore had to put in his eyebrow. Some stupid sergeant gave him a B.A.R. to tote during the war and he hauled it all over Europe until he finally got a medal for using it in the right place at the right time. Then he just went back to being Lippy Sullivan again with nobody except the Internal

Revenue Service and me ever knowing his real first name, and now he was dead.

So long, Lippy. Wish I had known you better. Maybe I will.

I had been in too many pads like this not to pick up the little signs. It wasn't what *was* there. It was what *wasn't*. There was that little Spartan touch that flipped you right back into an Army barracks where what you had you kept in your pocket. Lippy had been here almost two years and he hadn't collected anything at all. The shade on the lamp had been patched and painted to match the fabric, the old chair in the corner had been repaired where it was possible and the cracks in the plastered walls had been grouted to keep the roaches contained and the drafts out.

The one cupboard held an assortment of chili, hash, a half-dozen eggs, some canned vegetables, two boxes of salt and an oversized can of pepper. Lippy didn't exactly live high off the hog. But then again, he didn't ask for much, either. He sure didn't ask to get killed.

I took my time and went through his stuff piece by piece and wound up wondering what he had that made him valuable enough to die like he did. There wasn't one damn place he could have hidden anything and not the slightest sign that he even tried.

Yet somebody had sliced him up to make him talk.

Without thinking I sat on the edge of his bed, then stretched out and folded my hands behind my head and looked at the ceiling. It was a lousy bed but a lot better than what we had in the Army sometimes. Come on, Lippy, what was it? Did you have something? Did you *see* something? Why remember my phone number?

I let a curse slip across my lips because Lippy himself had given me the answer. What was it? Yeah ... *"No reason, Mike ... no reason."* And at a time like that a guy just doesn't lie.

But he had called for me and without having to say it, told me not to let him go out like that, a nothing nobody with a first name the world would never remember, but with that single phone call he had begged me not to let him be just another statistic in the massive book of records the great city keeps for its unrecognizables.

All right, Lippy. You are a somebody. Get off my back, will you? Maybe you didn't think there was a reason, but somebody else sure as hell had a good one for killing you.

I slid off the bed and picked my hat off the floor, then got to my feet and walked to the door. To the empty room I said, "Mike, you're getting old. The edge is off. You're missing something. It's right here and you're missing it."

The super popped the door open before I even knocked. I walked in past him to the couch against the wall, pulled the cushions off and unzipped the covers. Inside was a foam rubber pad and nothing else. I turned it over and felt around the burlap and canvas bottom, but there was nothing there either. I knew the cops had gone through the same routine so I wasn't really expecting to find anything anyway. When I finished I left it like it was and looked at the slob with the half-empty beer can who was hating me with his eyes. "Put it back where you got it," I said.

"Look, I had to clean . . ."

"I'll clean *you*, buddy. I'll turn you inside out and let the whole neighborhood watch while I'm doing it."

"Nobody even paid me . . ."

"You want it now?" I asked him.

The beer can fell out of his hand and he belched. Another second and he was going to get sick.

"Put it back," I told him again.

Jenkins and Wiley were ten minutes away from being off duty, having coffee in Raul Toulé's basement hideaway. I pulled a chair out with my foot, waved for Raul to bring me a beer and sat down. Jenkins curled his beefy face up into a grin, and said, "Ain't it great being a private investigator? He don't have to drink coffee. He gets a beer. Just like that. How's it going, Mike?"

"So-so. I just came out of Lippy's place."

Wiley nodded and took a sip of coffee. "Yeah, we got the word. Mumpy Henley spotted you getting out of the cab. Ever since you busted him on that assault rap he'd like to peg you. Doing anything illegal, Mike?"

"Certainly."

"That's good. Just do it to the right people."

"I try." I took my beer from Raul and downed half of it. "You guys get anything?"

Jenkins ran his hand through his mop of hair and shook his head. "Dead end. You know what we got in an eight-block area this past month? Four kills, eight rapes, fourteen burglaries and nine muggings. That's just what was reported."

"Should keep you guys pretty busy."

"Natch. We solved six murders, none of the rapes

20

wanted to prosecute, two burglars were apprehended, one by an old woman with a shotgun and another by Sid Cohen's kid ... and those two bragged about a hundred something they pulled around here. Only that crazy Swede policewoman nailed a mugger. She broke his arm. Nice place to live, but don't try to visit."

I said, "What about Lippy?"

Wiley fingered some potato chips out of the bowl in front of him and stuffed them in his mouth. "Not a damn thing. His employers vouch for him, the few neighborhood places he did business with give him an okay, nobody can figure out any reason why he should have been knocked off like that, so what's to say? Most everybody around here thinks it was some nut. It wouldn't have been the first time."

"How long you figure on staying on it?" I asked them.

"Not much left to do unless we get a break," Jenkins said. "Now we wait. If it was a psycho he'll probably hit again. Trouble is with that kind, you never know what they're going to do."

"It wasn't any psycho," I told him quietly.

They both looked at me, waiting.

"Just something I feel," I added. "You saw the lab reports. The place was searched."

"For what?" Wiley finished his coffee and pushed his cup away. "Your friend didn't have anything worth looking for."

"Somebody thought he did."

"Well, if they make anything out of those two sets of prints, we may get lucky. Look, I'm going to call in. Who's buying?"

I grinned at him and picked up the tab. Wiley fished a dime out of his pocket and went to the phone booth while I paid the bill. When he came back he had an amused frown on his face. "You could have been right, Mike."

"Oh?"

"Lippy did have something worth looking for only it wasn't in his room. Captain Chambers took a flyer and checked the local banks. Lippy had over twenty-seven hundred bucks in the Commerce National. Odd deposits every so often. No specific amounts."

"Nobody found a bankbook on him," I said.

"It was in his locker where he worked. He had it stuck under a batch of order forms. So now we have a motive."

"Murder for that kind of money?" I asked him.

"Hell, around here you could buy a dozen kills for that."

Siderman's Wholesale Groceries was a busy little place filled with the tangy odors of a farmhouse pantry with all the activity of an anthill. Young Joe Siderman led me back to his office, tossed me an apple and told me to sit down.

"Tough about Lippy," he said. "He was a good guy. They know who did it yet?"

I shook my head. "The police think somebody knew about that twenty-seven hundred he had saved up and maybe had it in his room."

"Crazy world, ain't it?"

"You see that bankbook of his?"

"Sure, I found it in his stuff. Nobody woulda known about it for months maybe if that Captain Chambers didn't get me poking around for it."

"Remember any of the deposits?"

"You know me, Mike. I'm a nosy bastard, so sure, I took a look. Like mostly from ten to fifty bucks each time. No special dates of deposits though. Sometimes twice a week, sometimes once."

"Lippy make that much here?"

Joe shined his apple on his sleeve and took a bite of it. "So we pay minimum wages for his job. It wasn't exactly skilled help. Lippy took home maybe sixty bucks a week. He never made no complaints about it. I don't know how he coulda saved that much these days. He didn't handle no cash here so he wasn't hitting the till. Maybe he played the horses."

"Nobody's that lucky, Joe."

"He got it from somewhere."

"Think maybe one of the others he worked with would know?"

"Doubt it. He got along good with everybody, but he never really buddied up to nobody special."

"Screwy," I said. "Why would he keep a bankbook stashed here?"

"That ain't unusual," Joe told me. "Half these guys what live in furnished rooms ain't got no families and think the job's their home. A coupla guys keep everything in their lockers here. Hell, Lippy even had his Army discharge and his rent receipts in that box. You want me to ask around a little? Maybe somebody knew him better than I thought."

"I'd appreciate it," I said. I tossed one of my business cards on his desk. "You can reach me here if anything turns up."

22

"Sure. Want another apple? They're pretty good. Come from upstate."

"Next time. Thanks for the talk."

I got up and started for the door when Joe stopped me. "Hey, one thing, Mike."

"What's that?"

"Was Lippy livin' with a broad?"

"Not that I know of. He never played around. Why?"

"Just something funny I thought of. We sell the help groceries at wholesale, you know? So always they buy just so much on payday. A few weeks back that Lippy doubled his order three weeks running then cut back down again."

"He ever do that before?"

"Nope, but I'll tell you something. It didn't surprise me none. You know what I think? He was always a soft touch and he was feeding somebody who was harder up than he was. Like I said, he was a nice guy."

"Yeah. So nice that somebody killed him."

"Times are tough all over."

The haze over the city had solidified into lumpy gray masses and you could smell the rain up there. I picked up the afternoon paper at a newsstand on Broadway and went into the Automat for coffee. Upstairs at an empty table I went through both sections of the edition without finding anything on Lippy at all. Tom-Tom Schneider was getting a heavy play, but he was a big hood in the policy racket, handling all the uptown collections. Be honest, I thought, be forgotten. Convicted criminals who bought two .38 slugs in the brain for crossing the wrong man get the big splash. At least they go out with everybody knowing their names. Even then, old Tom-Tom was being crowded a little by the political news, the latest Met scores and a mystery death in the Times Square subway station.

Somebody behind me said, "Hello, Mike, doing your homework?"

I looked over my shoulder and grinned. Eddie Dandy from WOBY–TV was standing there with a tray of milk and two kinds of pie, looking more like a saloon swamper than a video news reporter.

"You got my favorite table," he said.

I pushed a chair out for him. "Be my guest. I thought you guys ate free in all the best places in town."

"You get tired of gourmet foods, kid. I go for a little home cooking now and then. Besides, this place is closest to the job."

"Someday you're going to shave and wear an unwrinkled suit in the daytime and nobody's going to know you," I told him. "A dandy you are by name only."

Eddie put his pie and milk down, set the tray on the empty table beside us and picked up his fork. "That's what the wife keeps telling me. We people in show business like to change characters."

"Yeah, sure."

Between bites he said, "Petie Canero saw you down at headquarters. That Sullivan thing, wasn't it?"

I nodded and took another pull at my coffee. "It's still cold."

"You got to be a big man to get any action nowadays. Like Schneider. They'll spend a bundle going after his killers and wind up with nothing anyway."

"Maybe not."

"Oh hell, it was a contract kill. Somebody hired an out-of-town hit man and that was it for Tom-Tom. He's been stepping on too many toes trying to get on top. Everybody saw it coming. For one thing, he steps outside without his two musclemen beside him and it's bingo time. The cops ask questions but who's going to talk?"

"Somebody always does."

"When it's too late to move in. Right now I wish somebody would say something about that body in the subway. I never saw such a damn cover-up in my life. We all got the boot at the hospital ... nice and polite, but the big boot just the same. What gets me is ... ah, hell."

I frowned and looked across the table at him. "Well ... what about it?"

"Nothing. Just that coincidences make me feel funny."

"Afraid I'll scoop you on your own program?"

Eddie finished his first piece of pie, washed it down with half a glass of milk and reached for the other. "Sure, man," he grinned. "No, it's just funny, is all. Remember when I did the news for the Washington, D.C., station? Well, I got to know a lot of the local citizenry. So when I went down to the hospital I spotted a couple of familiar faces. One was Crane from the State Department. He said one of his staff was in with an appendectomy and he was visiting. Then I saw Matt Hollings."

"Who's Hollings?"

"Remember that stink about the train loaded with containers of nerve gas out West ... the stuff they were going to dump in the ocean only they wouldn't let it travel across the country?"

"Yeah."

"Hollings was in charge of the project originally," Eddie

said. "So when I saw Hollings and Crane talking I checked on Crane's friend. She was there with an appendectomy, all right, but she was a young girl in the steno pool who had only been with State six weeks. Seems funny they could have gotten that close in such a short time."

"She could have been a relative."

"Unlikely. The girl was a native Puerto Rican."

"Guys and gals are a strange combination," I said.

"Not with a wife like Crane's. Anyway, it was a coincidence and I don't like coincidences. They get admittance, we get the boot. All because some bum twitches to death on a subway platform. If they got a make on him it wouldn't have been so bad, but there was no identification at all."

"It's a shame you guys work so hard for a story," I laughed.

Eddie finished his pie and milk, belched gently and got up. "Back to the grind, buddy. I got to get my garbage ready for tonight."

I looked at him, nodded silently and watched him leave. Eddie Dandy had just told me what I had forgotten. Damn, I thought.

Outside it had started to rain.

The kid perched on the steps of the brownstone lifted the cardboard box off his head and peered up at me. The super, he said, went down to the deli for his evening six-pack of beer. From there he'd go to Welch's Bar, have a few for starters, tell some lies and make a pass at Welch's barmaid before he came home. That wouldn't be for another hour yet. Smart, these kids. Twelve going on thirty. I tossed him a quarter and he put the box back on his head so he could listen to the rain hammer on it and ignored me.

I didn't bother to wait for the super. I went to the back of the hallway, found the stairs to the basement and snapped my penlight on. I had to pick my way around the clutter of junk to the bottom, then climb over trash that had been accumulating for years before I came to the current collection. Four banged up, rusted cans, each half filled with garbage, were nested beside the crumbling stairwell that led to the backyard and the areaway to the street. Tomorrow was collection day.

Garbage. The residue of a man. Sometimes it could tell you more than what he saved.

I turned the cans over and kicked the contents around on the floor, separating the litter with my foot. A rat ran out over my toe and scurried away into the darkness. Empty cans, crumpled boxes and newspaper made up most of the contents, the decayed food smell half obscured by the fumes from some old paint-soaked rags at the bottom of one can. A fire inspector would flip over that. There was a pile of sticky sawdust in a stained shopping bag that was all that was left of Lippy. It almost made me gag. Farther down was some broken glass, two opened envelopes and a partially crushed shoebox. The envelopes were addressed to Lipton Sullivan. One was a notice from the local political organization encouraging him to vote for their candidate in the next election. The other was a mimeographed form letter from a furniture store listing their latest sale items.

I tossed them back and picked up the box, ripping the folded-in top back with my fingers.

Then I was pretty sure I knew where all of Lippy's bank deposit money had been coming from. The box was loaded with men's wallets and some goodies that obviously came from a woman's purse. There was no money anywhere.

My old friend Lippy had been a damn pickpocket.

Velda was already at my apartment when I got there, curled up like a sleek cat at the end of the sofa, all lovely long legs that the miniskirt couldn't begin to hide and a neckline it didn't try to. Those gorgeous breasts were still high and bouncy, flaring out in a wild challenge, her stomach flat until it took that delicious swell outward into her thighs and always that silky pageboy of auburn hair framing a face that was much too pretty for anybody's good.

"You look obscene," I said.

"It's a very studied pose," she reminded me. "It's supposed to have an effect on you."

"And it does, kitten. You know me." I tossed the box on the coffee table.

"Why don't you get out of those wet clothes and then we'll talk."

"Don't mind the garbage smell," I said. "It's a dirty business. Make me a drink and take a look at that stuff. Don't touch anything. I'm going to take a hot shower. This racket is beginning to get to me."

The impish grin she had greeted me with was lost in the look of concern and she nodded. I walked into the bedroom, peeled off my coat, yanked the .45 from the shoulder rig, tossed it on the dresser and got rid of the rest of

26

my clothes. I spent fifteen minutes under a stinging needle spray, got out, wrapped a towel around my middle and walked back into the living room trailing wet footsteps.

Velda handed me my drink, the ice clinking in the glass. "Now you look obscene. Why don't you ever dry yourself off?"

"That's what I got you for," I said.

"Not me. I'd only make you wetter."

"Someday I'm going to marry you and legalize all this nonsense."

"You know how long I've been hearing that?"

I tasted the drink. She'd hit the blend right on the button. "At least you're engaged," I said.

"The longest one on record." I grinned at her and she smiled back. "That's okay, Mike. I'm patient." Her eyes drifted toward the box on the table. She had dumped out the contents and sorted things out with the end of a ball-point pen. "Sorry about Lippy, Mike. Pretty disappointing. I always had him figured for a right guy."

"He gave that impression," I said. "What do you make of it?"

"Plain enough. Somebody knew what he did in his spare time and tried to heist his take. He wouldn't tell where he hid it because it wouldn't have done any good since it was in the bank. So he was killed. Getting rid of the stuff is part of the pattern. They take the money and dump the rest. He probably could have tried using some of the credit cards in those wallets, but that doesn't fit a pickpocket's usual routine."

"Sure looks that way."

"You go through any of that yet, Mike?"

"I didn't have time. Why?"

"Because Lippy didn't hit just anybody. That's the money crowd you see there. Wait until you check it out. If Lippy was a working dip he wouldn't be allowed inside their circles. He even got to a woman."

"I saw that compact."

"Gold with real diamonds. Expensive, but not pawnable."

"Why not?"

"Look at the hallmark and the inscription. It's a Tiffany piece given to Heidi Anders."

"The actress?"

"The same. The donor signed himself Bunny, so we'll assume it's Bunny Henderson with whom she's been seen these last few months. Playboy, jet setter, ne'er do well, but carries a load of power in his back pocket."

27

"What's it worth?" I asked her.

"My guess about five thousand. But that would be nothing to her. She's loaded with gems. To her that compact was more utilitarian than ornamental. I'm surprised a pickpocket specializing in wallets would tap a woman's handbag."

"Women aren't generally wallet carriers, kitten. He could have gotten a handful of money and that at the same time."

"Your buddy got plenty." She nodded toward the table. "Check it."

I walked over and took a look at some of the wallets she had spread open. All of them were expensive leather items, the plastic windows filled with top-rated credit cards. I picked up a pen and turned a few of them over, then stopped and tapped the inside of the large pigskin job. The top half of two pink pieces of cardboard were sticking up out of the slot. "There's your answer, kid. Theater tickets. He was working the new Broadway openings. Those ducats are being scalped at fifty bucks a pair which is a little more than the ordinary workingman can afford."

"Mike ... those bank deposits. They weren't all that big."

"Because the people he was hitting didn't work with cash. They're all on the credit card system. But at least he knew he was always sure of something."

"You missed something, Mike."

"Where?"

Velda pointed to the worn black morocco case at the end. "He didn't have any credit cards, but there's a driver's license, some club memberships and a very interesting name on all of them."

I finished half my drink, put my glass down and studied the wallet. Ballinger. Woodring Ballinger. Woody Ballinger to his friends and the cops alike. Big-time spender, old-time hood who ran a tight operation nobody could get inside of.

"Great," I said.

"He could have run Lippy down and put some heat on him."

"Not Woody. He wouldn't take the chance. Not any more. He'd lose his dough and let it go at that."

"So it had to be someone who knew what Lippy was doing."

"Pat still has two sets of prints he's checking on."

"What will you do with this stuff?"

"Take it down to Pat tomorrow and let them process it. The suckers will be glad to get their credit cards back."

"Mike ..."

"What?"

"You could have brought this right to Pat, you know."

"Yeah, I know. And they could have gone to the trouble of poking around in Lippy's garbage too."

"That puts you right in the middle. You're going to stick your neck out again."

"Something's too off balance for me. If Lippy were big enough they'd be giving this a rush job like they are with Tom-Tom Schneider. Everything gets priority when you're a big name. So now Lippy goes down in the books as a pickpocket knocked off for his loot. Maybe one day they'll get his killer on another charge. End of story."

"But not for you."

"Not for me."

Velda shook her head and gave a mock sigh. "All right, I took down the names and addresses of everybody heisted. The list is over there." She pointed to a half-used steno pad on the TV set.

"You always try to outthink me, don't you?"

"Generally," she said. A smile started in the corner of her eyes.

"Know what I'm thinking right now?"

With a quick motion of her hand she reached out and flipped the towel from around my waist and let it fall to the floor. Those beautiful full lips parted in the rest of the smile and she said, "Yes, I know what you're thinking."

CHAPTER 3

Pat made a big production out of the glare he was giving me, but the edge was all mine because his group should have found the stuff in the first place, not me. It's great to be public-spirited, but not when you're soaking wet, stinking from cellar garbage and alone with a beautiful broad.

He finally said, "Okay, Mike, you're off the hook, but you can still get a stinger up your tail if the D.A.'s office decides to probe."

"So cover for me," I told him. "Now, any of that stuff reported missing?"

Pat flipped through the report sheets on his desk and nodded. "Practically all of it. The credit cards have been canceled, two license renewals have been applied for and you'll be three hundred dollars richer. Reward money."

"Forget it. That way the D.A.'ll really nail it down. How about that compact?"

"Miss Heidi Anders thought she had mislaid it. She never reported it as missing or possibly stolen. Incidentally, it was well insured."

"Great to be rich. Did any of them know where the stuff was lifted?"

"Not specifically, but they all felt it was on the street somewhere. Three of them were positive it was in the theater area, William Dorn pinpointed his on Broadway outside of Radio City Music Hall. He had used his wallet money to pay off a cabbie and remembered being jostled in the crowd outside the theater. A block later he felt for the wallet and it was gone."

"How did Ballinger take it?"

Pat shrugged and put the reports back in the folder. "Surly as usual. He said he had a couple hundred bucks in his wallet that we could forget about. Getting his driver's license back is good enough. We can mail it to him."

"Nice guys are hard to find."

"Yeah," Pat said sourly. "Look, about those rewards. My advice is to take them before they insist and put through an inquiry that might attract attention." He tore a sheet off his memo pad and passed it to me. "Irving Grove, William Dorn, Reginald Thomas and Heidi Anders. There are the addresses. You don't exactly have to lie, but you don't *have* to mention you're not with the department."

"Hell, cops don't collect rewards."

"People are funny. They like to do favors too."

"I'll donate it to the Police Athletic League."

"Go ahead."

"What about Lippy, Pat?"

"Hard to figure people out, isn't it? You think you know them, then something like this happens. It isn't the first time. It won't be the last. Someday we'll nail the guy who did it. The file isn't closed on him. Meanwhile, just leave it alone. Don't bug yourself with it."

"Sure." I got up and tossed my raincoat over my shoulder. "Incidentally, any news on Tom-Tom Schneider?"

"He thumped his last thump. A contract kill. One of the slugs matched another used in a Philly job last month."

"Those boys usually dump their pieces after a hit."

"Maybe he was fond of it. It was nine millimeter Luger ammo. Those pieces are getting hard to come by."

"How'd you do with that body in the subway?" I asked him.

Pat's face stiffened and he stopped swinging in his chair. His eyes went cold and narrow and his voice had a bite to it. "What are you getting at, Mike?"

I stuck a cigarette in my mouth and held a match to it. "Just curious. You know how I pick up bits and pieces of information. New York isn't all that tight."

He didn't move, but I saw his knuckles whiten around the arms of his chair. "Buddy, how you get around is unbelievable. Why the curiosity?"

I took a guess and said, "Because you have every available man checking the guy out. Even some Feds have moved in, but when it comes to Lippy it's a one-day deal."

For a moment it looked like Pat was going to explode, then he looked at me, his mind trying to penetrate through mine to see if I was guessing or not. It was my mention of the Feds that put the frown back on his face again and he said, "Damn," very softly and let go the arms of the chair. "What do you know, Mike?"

31

"Want an educated opinion?"

"Never mind. It's better that you knew so you wouldn't be guessing in front of the wrong people."

I took a pull on the butt and blew a shaft of smoke in his direction. "So?"

"A sharp medic in the hospital didn't like the symptoms. They autopsied him immediately and confirmed their suspicions. He was infected by one of the newer and deadlier bacteria strains."

"Unusual?"

"This was. The culture was developed in government laboratories for C.G. Warfare only. They're not sure of the contagion factor and don't want to start a panic."

"Maybe he was a worker there."

"We're checking that out now. Anyway, just keep it to yourself. If this thing gets around we'll know the source it came from."

"You shouldn't be so trusting then."

"Oh, hell, get out of here, Mike."

I snubbed out the butt in his ashtray, grinned and went through the door. Eddie Dandy would give his left whoosis for this scoop, but I wasn't in the market for left whoosises.

I managed to reach Velda just before she went out to lunch and told her I wouldn't be in the rest of the day. She had already cleaned up most of the paperwork and before she could start in rearranging the furniture I said, "Look, honey, one thing you can do. Go to Lippy's bank and find the clerk he deposited that money with."

"Pat has a record of that."

"Yeah, of the amounts. What I want to know is if he remembered what denominations of bills were deposited."

"Important?"

"Who can tell? I'm just not satisfied with the answers, that's all. I'll check back with you later."

I hung up and went back into the afternoon rain. A couple were getting out of a cab on the corner and I grabbed it before anyone else could and told the driver where to go.

Woodring Ballinger had a showpiece office on the twenty-first floor of a Fifth Avenue building but he never worked there. His operating space was the large table in the northeast corner of Finero's Steak House just off Broadway, a two-minute walk to Times Square. There were three black phones and a white one in front of him and the two guys he was with were in their early thirties with the total businessman look. Only they both had police records dating back to their teens. That businessman look was one that Ballinger never could hope to buy. He tried hard enough, with three-hundred-buck suits and eighty-dollar shoes, but he still looked like he just came off a dock after pushing a dolly of steel around. Scar tissue laced his eyebrows and knuckles, he always needed a shave and seemed to have a perpetual sneer plastered on his mouth.

I said, "Hello, Woody."

He only half looked at me. "What the hell do you want?"

"Tell your boys to blow."

Both of them looked up at me a little amused. When I reached for my deck of cigarettes they saw the .45 in the holster and stopped being amused. Woody Ballinger said, "Go wait in the bar."

Obediently, they got up, went past me without another glance and pulled up stools at the bar with their backs to us. I sat down opposite Woody and waved the waiter over to bring me a beer.

"You lost, Hammer?"

"Not in this town. I live here. Or have you forgotten?" I gave him a dirty grin and when he scowled I knew he remembered, all right.

"Cut the crap. What d'you want?"

"You had your wallet lifted not long ago."

His fingers stopped toying with his glass. The waiter came, set the beer down and I sipped the head off it. "What's new about that? The cops found it."

"*I* found it," I said. "Yours wasn't the only one in the pile."

"So okay. I get my license back. There wasn't no money in it. The bum who lifted it grabbed that. Two hundred and twelve bucks. Where'd you find it?"

"Doesn't matter. The guy's dead who was holding it. Somebody carved him apart for nothing. The money was all in the bank."

"Hell, I'd sure like to get my hands on the bastard. Hittin' me, the dirty punk. Maybe he's better off." Woody stopped then, his eyes screwing half shut. "Why tell me about it anyway?"

"Because maybe you might know what dips are working the area. If you don't know, maybe you can find out."

"What for? If the guy's dead he . . ."

"Because I don't like to think it was the guy who was killed. So poke around. You know who to ask."

33

"Go ask them yourself, buster."

"No, you do it, Woody. I haven't got time." I finished my beer, threw a buck on the table and got up. When I went by the bar I tapped one of the business types on the shoulder and said, "You can go back now."

They just looked at me, picked up their drinks and went back to their boss without a word. Ballinger chose his people carefully.

It wasn't too long ago that the East Side past Lexington had been just one long slum section with a beautiful vitality all its own you couldn't duplicate anywhere in the world. Then they had torn down the elevated and let the light in and it was just too much for the brilliant speculators to miss.

Oh, the slums were still there, isolated pockets nestling shoulder to shoulder with the sterile facades of the expensive high rise apartments, tiny neighborhoods waiting for the slam of the iron ball to send them into an oblivion of plaster dust and crumpled bricks. If an inanimate thing could die, the city was dying of cancerous modernism. One civilization crawling over another. Then there would be ruins laid on top of ruins. I could smell the artificially cooled air seeping from the huge glassed doorways around the uniformed doormen and thought, hell, I liked it better the other way.

Miss Heidi Anders occupied 24C, a corner patio apartment on the good side of the building where the sun came in all day and you weren't forced to see how others lived just a ninety-degree turn away from you. The doorman announced me, saying it was in connection with the compact she had lost and I heard her resonant voice come right out of the wall phone and say, "Oh, yes, the policeman. Please send him up."

The doorman would have liked to mix a little small talk with me but the elevator was empty and I stepped inside, pushed number twenty-four and took the ride upstairs.

I had only seen production photos of Heidi Anders, commercial pictures in the flowing gowns she generally wore in the Broadway musicals. For some reason I had always thought of her as the big robust type who could belt a song halfway across the city without a mike. I wasn't quite ready for the pert little thing in the white hip-hugger slacks and red bandanna top that left her all naked in between. The slacks were cut so low there was barely enough hip left to hug them up. And if the knot on the bandanna top slipped even a fraction of an inch it was going to burst right off her. What got me, though, were the eyelashes she had painted around her navel. The damn thing seemed to be inspecting me.

All I could say was, "Miss Anders?"

She gave me a nervous little smile and opened the door all the way. "Yes . . . but please, call me Heidi. Everybody does. Come in, come in." Her tongue made a quick pass across her lips and her smile seemed a little forced. No wonder cops were lonely. Even if they thought you were one they got the jumps.

"Hammer. Mike Hammer."

She took my coat and hat, slipped them on a rack, then led me into the spacious living area of the apartment. She didn't walk. She had a gait all her own, a swaying, rolling, dancing motion that put all her muscles into play. Unconsciously, she flipped the lovely tousle of ash-blonde hair over her head, spun around with her arms spread in a grand theatrical gesture and said, "Home!"

It might have been home to her, but it looked like some crazy love nest to me. It was all pillows, soft couches and wild pictures, but it sure looked interesting. "Nice," I said.

She took a half jump into one of the overstuffed chairs and sank down into it. "Sit, Mr. Hammer. May I make you a drink? But then, policemen never drink on duty, do they?"

"Sometimes." I didn't trust the couch. I pulled an ottoman up and perched on the edge of it.

"Well, they never do on TV. Now, are you the one who found my compact?"

"Yes, Ma'am." I hoped it was the proper TV intonation.

Once again she gave me that nervous little smile. "You know, I never even realized I had lost it. I'm so glad it has been recovered. You're getting a reward, you know."

"I'd appreciate it if you'd just make a donation to the P.A.L."

"The Police Athletic League? Oh, I did a benefit for them one time. Certainly, if that's the way you want it. Do you have it with you?"

"No, you can pick it up from the property clerk after you've identified it. It's a Tiffany piece so they'll have a record of it and your insurance policy will have it described. No trouble getting it back."

Her shoulders gave an aggravated twitch, then she ran her fingers through her beautifully unruly hair and smiled again. "I don't know what I'm impatient about. I've been without it all this time, another day won't matter. I guess

35

it's just the excitement. I've never really been involved with the police except to get my club permit and that was years ago. They don't even do that any more now, do they?"

"No more. Look, maybe I will have that drink. Show me where the goodies are."

"Right behind you." She pointed. "I'll have a small Scotch on the rocks."

I got up, made the drinks, and when I got back she had changed from the chair to the couch looking like she was half hoping she was going to get raped. I hated to disappoint her, but I handed her the Scotch and took the ottoman again to try my tall rye and ginger. She toasted me silently, tasted her drink and nodded approvingly, then: "You know ... since you didn't bring my compact, and you won't accept any reward, was there something you wanted to talk to me about?"

"Not many of us get a chance to see a luscious actress in the flesh. So to speak," I added. Her navel was still looking at me.

"You're sweet, but you're lying," she smiled. She tasted her drink again, leaned forward and put it on the floor between her feet. The halter top strained uncertainly, but held.

I said, "I was hoping you might remember when and where you lost that thing."

"Oh, but I do. I didn't think about it at first, but when I put my mind to it I remember quite well."

I took another pull at my drink and waited, trying to keep my eyes off her belly.

"I went to the theater to catch Roz Murray in the opening of her new show. During the intermission I went to the powder room and found it gone. I never suspected that it had been stolen, but I'm always misplacing things anyway, and I supposed I had left it at home. I was sure of it when I found that two fifty dollar bills and some singles were gone too. I thought I had scooped some out of my drawer before I left, but I was in such a damn rush to meet Josie to make curtain time I could have pulled a boo-boo."

"How did you get to the theater?"

"Josie picked me up downstairs in a cab and paid the bill."

"And you never bothered checking for it later?"

"Oh, I kind of looked around. I always keep a few hundred dollars loose in the drawer and the rest was still there and I didn't bother to count it. I figured the compact was simply tucked away someplace else."

I rattled the ice around in the glass and tried the drink again. "One more thing. At any time that evening do you remember being crowded?"

"Crowded?"

"Hemmed in with people where somebody could make a pass at your handbag."

She looked thoughtful a moment, then reached down for her drink again. It was a very unsettling move. Over the glass her eyes touched mine and her tongue made that nervous gesture again, passing quickly over her lips. "No ... not really ... but, yes, while we were going in there was this one man ... well, he sort of cut across in front of us and had to excuse himself. He acted like he knew somebody on the other side of us."

"Can you describe him?"

She squinched her eyes and mouth shut tight for a good five seconds, then let her face relax. Her eyes opened and she nodded. "He was about average height ... smaller than you. In his late forties. Not well dressed or anything .. and he had funny hair."

"What kind of funny?"

"Well, he should have been gray but he wasn't and it grew back in deep V's on either side."

I knew it showed on my face. The drink turned sour in my mouth and that strange sensation seemed to crawl up my back. She had just described Lippy Sullivan.

"Is ... something wrong?"

I faked a new expression and shook my head. "No, everything is working out just right." I put the glass down and stood up. "Thanks for the drink."

Heidi Anders held out her hand and let me pull her up from the depths of the cushions. "I appreciate your coming like this. I only wish ..."

"What?"

"You could have brought the compact. Police stations scare me."

"Get me your insurance policy, a note authorizing me to pick it up for you, and you'll have it tomorrow."

For the first time a real smile beamed across her face. "Will you?" She didn't wait for an answer. She broke into that wild gait, disappeared into another room and was back in three minutes with both the things I asked for.

She walked me to the door and held my coat while I slipped into it. When I turned around her face was tilted up toward mine, her mouth alive and moist. "Since you wouldn't take the reward, let me give you one you *can* keep."

37

Very gently, she raised herself on her toes, her hands slipping behind my head. Those lips were all fire and mobility, her tongue a thing that quested provocatively. I could feel the hunger start and didn't want it to get loose, so just as gently I pushed her away, letting my hands slide down the satin nudity of her back until my fingertips rested on the top of those crazy hip huggers and my thumbs encircled her almost to those exotic areas where there is no turning back. I heard her breath catch in her throat and felt the muscles tauten, her skin go damp under my palms, then I let her go.

"That was mean," she said.

"So is painting that eye around your belly button."

The throaty laugh bubbled up again and she let her hands ease down from my neck and across my chest. Then the laugh stopped as she felt the .45 under my coat, and that nervous little glint was back in her eyes.

"Tomorrow," I said.

"Tomorrow, Mike." But she said it like she really didn't mean it at all.

The afternoon papers were still splashing the death of Tom-Tom Schneider all over their pages. The D.A.'s office was running a full-scale investigation into all his affairs and connections, the State Committee on Organized Crime had just been called into executive session for another joust at the underworld and anybody with a political ax to grind was making his points with the reporters. Everybody seemed agreed that it was a contract kill and two columnists mentioned names of known enemies and were predicting another gangland war.

Someplace there would be another meeting and the word would go out to put a big cool on activities until the heat had died down and someplace else a contract was being paid off and spent.

Lippy Sullivan had been forgotten. Maybe it was just as well. The guy who died on the subway station wasn't mentioned at all either. When I finished with the paper I tossed it in the litter basket and went into the cigar store on the corner and called Velda.

When she came on I asked her how she made out at the bank and she said, "The teller remembered Lippy all right, Mike. Seemed like they always had a little something to talk about."

"He remember the deposits?"

"Uh-huh. Tens, twenties and singles. Nothing any bigger. From what was said he gathered that Lippy was in some small business enterprise by himself that paid off in a minor fashion."

"Nothing bigger than a twenty?"

"That's what he told me. Oh, and he always had it folded with a rubber band around it as if he were keeping it separate from other bills. Make anything out of it?"

"Yeah. He was smart enough to cash in the big ones before depositing them so nothing would look funny." I told her briefly about Heidi Anders identifying Lippy in the crowd.

All she said was a sorrowful, "Oh, Mike."

"Tough."

"Why don't you leave it alone?"

"I don't like things only half checked out, kid. I'll push it a little bit further, then dump it. I wish to hell he hadn't even called me."

"Maybe you won't have to go any further."

"Now what?"

"Pat called about twenty minutes ago. He had pictures of Lippy circulating around the theater areas all day. Eight people recalled having seen him in the area repeatedly."

"Hell, he lived not too far from there."

"Since when was Lippy a stage fan? He never even went to the neighborhood movie house. You know what his habits were."

"Okay, okay. Were they reliable witnesses?"

"Pat says they were positive ID's. Someplace Lippy learned a new trade and found a good place to work it."

"Nuts."

"So make Pat sore at you. He's hoping this new bit will keep you out of their routine work. Now, is there any reason why you still have to go after it?"

"Damn right. Only because Lippy said there wasn't any reason to begin with."

"Then what else can I do?"

"Go ask questions around Lippy's place. Do your whore act. Maybe somebody'll open up to you who won't speak to me or the cops."

"In that neighborhood?"

"Just keep your price up and you won't have any trouble."

She swore at me and I grinned and hung up.

I was only three blocks away from Irving Grove's Men's Shop on Broadway and there was still time to make it before the office buildings started disgorging their daily meals of humans, so I ducked back into the drizzle and walked to the corner. A little thunder rumbled overhead, but there were a few breaks in the smog layers and it didn't look like the rain was going to last much longer. In a way, it was too bad. The city was always a little quieter, a little less crowded and a lot more friendly when it was wet.

Irving Grove was typical of the Broadway longtimers. Short, stocky, harried, but smiling and happy to be of service. He turned the two customers over to his clerks and ushered me into his cubicle of an office to one side of his stockroom, cleared a couple of chairs of boxes and invoices and drew two coffees from the battered urn on the desk.

"You know, Mr. Hammer, it is a big surprise to know my wallet was found. Twice before this has happened, but never do I get them back. It wasn't the money. Three hundred dollars I can afford, but all those papers. Such trouble."

"I know the feeling."

"And you are sure there will be no reward?"

"The P.A.L., remember?"

He gave me a shrewd smile and a typical gesture of his head. "But you are not with the police force, of course. It would be nothing if . . ."

"You don't know me, Mr. Grove."

"Perhaps not personally, but I read. I know of the things you have done. Many times. In a way I am jealous. I work hard, I make a good living, but never any excitement. Not even a holdup. So I read about you and . . ."

"Did you ever stop to think that there are times I envy you?"

"Impossible." He stopped, the coffee halfway to his mouth. "Really?"

"Sometimes."

"Then maybe I don't feel so bad after all. It is better to just read, eh?"

"Much better," I said. "Tell me, are you a theater-goer?"

"No, only when my wife drags me there. Maybe once a year if I can't get out of it. Why?"

"Whoever lifted your wallet was working the theater crowds."

Irving Grove nodded sagely. "Ah, yes. That is possible. I see what you mean." He put his cup down and picked a half-smoked cigar from an ashtray and lit it. "See, Mr. Hammer, I live on the West Side. For years yet, always the same place. I close here and on nice nights I walk

40

home. Maybe a twenty-minute walk. Sometimes I go down one street, sometimes another, just to see the people, the excitement. You understand?"

I nodded.

"So pretty often I go past the theaters just when they're going in. I watch what they're wearing. It helps for my trade, you know. It was one of those nights when my wallet was stolen. I didn't even realize it until the next morning, and I couldn't be sure until I came back to the store to make sure I hadn't dropped it here somewhere." Right away I reported it and canceled all my credit cards."

"What denomination bills did you have with you?"

"Two one hundred dollar bills, a fifty and one five. That I remember. I always remember the money."

"Where did you carry it?"

"Inside my coat pocket."

I said, "Maybe you can remember anybody that pushed or shoved you that night. Anybody who was close to you in the crowd who could have lifted it?"

Grove smiled sadly and shook his head. "I'm afraid I'm not a very suspicious person, Mr. Hammer. I never look at faces, only clothes. No, I wouldn't remember that."

I crushed my paper cup, tossed it in the wastebasket and thanked him for his time. He was just another blank in a long series of blanks and all it was doing was making Lippy look worse than ever. Velda was right. I should have just left it all alone.

So I got out of there, walked over to Forty-fourth and The Blue Ribbon, pulled out the chair behind my usual table and had the waiter bring me a knockwurst and beer. Jim waved hello from behind the bar and switched on the TV so I could watch the six o'clock news.

Eddie Dandy came on after the weather, freshly shaven, his usual checkered sportscoat almost eyestraining to watch whenever he moved, his voice making every piece of dull information sound like a world-shattering event. George came over and sat down with his ever-present coffee cup in his hand and started in on his favorite subject of food. He had just asked me about a new specialty he was thinking of putting on the menu when I stopped him short with a wave of my hand.

Eddie Dandy had changed the tone of his voice. He wasn't reading from his notes, he was looking directly into the camera in deadly seriousness and said, ". . . and once again the public is being kept in the dark about a matter of grave importance. The unidentified body found in the

Times Square station of the subway has been secretly autopsied with the findings kept locked in government files. No information has been given either the police or the press and the doctors who performed the autopsy are being confined in strict quarantine at this moment. It is this reporter's opinion that this man died of a virulent disease developed by this government's chemical-germ warfare research, one that could possibly lead to severe epidemic proportions, but rather than inform the public and institute an immediate remedial program, they chose to avoid panic and possible political repercussions by keeping this matter completely in the dark. Therefore, I suggest . . ."

I said, "Oh, shit!" Then threw a bill on the table and dashed to the phone booth in the next room. I threw a dime in the slot, dialed Pat's number and waited for him to come on the phone.

I said, "Mike here, Pat."

He was silent a second, then through his breathing he told me, "Get your ass down here like now, buddy. Like right this damn minute."

CHAPTER 4

Pat wouldn't talk to me. He didn't even want to look at me and for the first time since we had been friends I felt like telling him to go to hell. I didn't. I just sat there beside him in the patrol car and watched the streets roll by on the way to the office building on Madison Avenue where the watchdogs had their cute little front they thought nobody knew about. And this time even Pat was surprised when I got out first, went inside to the elevator and punched the 4 button without being told. There was a NO SMOKING sign in the elevator so I took out my deck, shook a cigarette loose and struck a wooden kitchen match across the NO. Then he knew how I felt too. He started to say something, only I got there first.

"You should have asked me," I said.

The others were all waiting, quiet and deadly, their faces full of venom, tinged with total dislike and anticipating selective revenge. *Screw them too,* I thought.

There weren't any introductions. The big guy with the bulging middle and the florid face simply pointed to a chair and after I looked at it long enough and decided on my own to sit down, I sat, then spun my butt into the middle of their big, beautiful mahogany company table and grinned when another one glared at me a second before picking it up and dropping it in a huge ceramic ashtray.

Everyone sat down with such deliberate motion you'd think we were about to go into a discussion of a successful bond issue. But it wasn't like that and I wasn't about to let them open the meeting. I waited until the last chair had scraped into position and said, "If you clowns think you're about to steamroller me, you'd just better start thinking straight. Nobody asked me here, nobody advised me of my rights, and right now I'd just as soon kick any or all of you on your damn tails ... including my erstwhile buddy

43

here ... and all you need to start the action is one little push."

"You're not under arrest, Hammer," the fat one said.

"Believe it, buddy, that I'm not. But I'm sure interested in getting that way."

When they looked at each other wondering what kind of a cat they had caught in their trap I knew I had the bull on them and I wasn't about to let go. For the first time I looked directly at Pat. "I saw Eddie Dandy's show tonight myself. You've already been informed by Captain Chambers here that I was a recipient of confidential information. It was given me in way of explanation so I wouldn't do any loose talking, so I assume everyone here figures I picked up a few fast bucks by passing that information on. Okay, right now, hear this just once. It was Eddie Dandy who suggested the idea and I just made a few discreet inquiries that shook up my good pal Pat to the point where he had to fill me in on the rest." I tapped out another butt and lit it. Somebody shoved the ashtray my way. "Pat, I said nothing, you got that?"

He was still the cop. His expression didn't change an iota. "Sorry, Mike."

"Okay, forget it."

"It can't be forgotten," the fat guy said. "Do you know who we are?"

"Who the hell are you trying to kid?" I asked him. "You're all D.C. characters playing political football with something you can't handle. Now you got Eddie Dandy on your backs and can't get him off."

One of the others snapped a pencil in two and stared at me, his face tight with rage. "He'll be here to explain his part in this."

"There *isn't* any part, you nut. All you can do now is offer excuses or start lying. Which is it? Or do you discredit Eddie? Tell me, is it true?"

Everybody wanted to talk at once, but the fat guy at the end silenced them with one word. Then he looked down the table at me and folded his hands with all the innocence of a bear trap. "Tell me, Mr. Hammer, why are you so militant?"

"Because I don't dig you goons. You're all bureaucratic nonsense, tax happy, self-centered socialistic slobs who think the public's a game you can run for your own benefit. One day you'll realize that it's the individual who pulls the strings, not committees."

"And you're that individual?"

"I can pull more than strings, friend, that's why you got

44

me here. Right now I'm all for going out and really sounding off about what I know. How about that?" I sat back and listened to the quiet.

Pat broke the eerie stillness. "Don't push him, Mr. Crane. The whole thing shook me for a minute, but I'd rather have him on our side."

"Protecting yourself, Captain?"

"Another remark like that and you'll be protecting yourself, Mr. Crane. I'll rap you right in the mouth."

The big man from the State Department took one look at Pat's face and the knuckles of his interlocking fingers whitened. "Captain . . ."

"You'll be better off just telling him, Mr. Crane. He isn't kidding."

They could talk with their eyes, this bunch. They could just look at each other and have a conversation, hash the problem out and come to a decision. When it was made, Crane gave an almost imperceptible nod and stared at me again, his eyes cold. "Very well. I don't approve, but considering how far out on a limb we are, we'll give you the story."

"Why?" I asked.

"Simply because we can't afford to have anyone prying into this affair. After Eddie Dandy's report we'll have everyone in the news media asking questions. They don't like negative answers. They'll go directly to Dandy and we're hoping you can influence him to state that he was wrong in his premises."

"Brother!" I snubbed my butt out and sat back in my chair. "You don't know reporters very well, do you? Where is Eddie now?"

"Being briefed on the incident. He'll be here shortly."

"You better have something good to tell him. Or me."

Crane nodded. "I think we have."

"I'm listening."

"Of course you realize the confidential nature of this matter?"

"I did before," I said.

Mr. Crane managed a little of his State Department pomp and leaned back, mentally choosing his words. When he was satisfied, he said, "In 1946 a Soviet agent was planted in this country by the regime then in power with specific instructions that at a certain time, when the economic and political factors were right, to totally sabotage certain key cities through the use of biological or chemical means. His orders were irrevocable. He was given the properties to accomplish his mission, and the

45

persons he could contact who would relay the schedule of destruction. This was a top secret project that could in no way be canceled out. This agent had one contact who, like him, was only to relay the information of when it would take place, then set in motion the machinery that would take over after the destruction finished our present system of government."

"And that guy is dead," I said.

"Very dead. Now we know the system he used. It was bacteriological. He's set everything in motion. It's a time delay affair. Unfortunately, he somehow got exposed himself and died."

I looked over at Pat. "You said it came out of our labs."

Crane didn't let him answer. "All research seems to come to the same conclusions. The strain of bacteria was similar, but not identical."

"You got troubles, Mr. Crane, haven't you? We have ICBM's, Polaris, all the new goodies stored up in silos around the country that can reach anywhere around the world, and now that you know what's on our necks we can get in there for a first strike, only you're not striking. Why?"

That caught them a little off base. Maybe they thought I couldn't figure it out. Crane gave me a perceptive brush of his eyes and said, "Because the Soviets are caught on their own horns. They don't want it either. They want it stopped right now and they're cooperating. There's a new regime in power and their entire political system has been changed in view of the Chinese situation. They can't afford to be hit from both sides. Only one of their personnel was able to hint at this development, but that was enough to get leads, process them and get the story. Do you see now why we can't afford a panic?"

"So you're buying time."

"Exactly."

Before he could answer another of the gray flannel boys came in, walked up and spoke to him. Crane nodded and said, "Bring him in."

Eddie Dandy looked like he had been wrung out in an old Maytag. Sweat had plastered his hair to his forehead, his sports jacket was rumpled and he couldn't keep his hands still at all. But his face still bore that hard stamp of the veteran newscaster with the "show me or else" look. Apparently they hadn't mentioned me to him at all and his eyes registered momentary surprise when he saw me sit-

46

ting there. I waved nonchalantly and winked and I knew damn well things were beginning to add up to him.

They gave him the same rundown they gave me, but he had saved up his little shocker for them. When Crane insisted just a little too hard on Eddie divulging his source of information, he simply said, "Why it was you and Mr. Hollings who tipped me off." I applauded with a laugh nobody appreciated. Pat gave me a tap with his foot.

"Please don't think everybody is stupid," Eddie told them. "I have to research news items and the death of that guy in the subway had certain earmarks that were familiar to me. Or did you forget the death of all those sheep out west when that nerve gas went in the wrong direction? Or the two lab workers whose families raised such hell about the cover-up when they kicked off? Seeing you two in the hospital was all it took to pin the probability down . . . that and a few inquiries made to knowledgeable scientists who don't approve of the more sophisticated methods of modern warfare."

Somehow they all seemed to stop communicating then. Their exchanges of looks didn't bring any responses. Redfaced, Crane mustered all his eloquence and put the proposition right on the line. Eddie could be the turning point of panic. Until the location of the destruct cannisters could be determined and destroyed, Eddie was to retract his broadcast and maintain that position.

He looked at me and I shrugged. I said, "There's a possiblity a mass search for the stuff might help."

"You'll get mass exodus from the cities and panic, Mr. Hammer," Crane told me. "No, we have competent people experienced in these matters and with help from the Soviets I'm confident it can be accomplished."

"Sure, you trust the Soviets and you know what you'll get. You get screwed every time and you slobs are all afraid of screwing back. What happens if you *don't* find the stuff?"

"We're not even considering that possiblity," he shot back. "No . . ."

But Eddie cut him off right there. "You're forgetting something. Now my neck is out with the network and the audience. I'll be coming off looking like a bumbling amateur. I'll be lucky if I can hang on to my job. So we make a deal."

"Yes?"

"No other reporter, broadcaster or what-have-you gets any part of this story if you pull it off. All I need is a hint that this has been leaked and I'll blow the whole thing all over your faces. *If* you manage to lock this thing up, I get first crack at releasing it along with verbal progress reports in the meantime. You haven't got much choice, so you can take it or leave it."

"We'll take it, Mr. Dandy," Crane said. This time the communication was complete. Everybody else agreed too.

Pat took Eddie Dandy and me to a late supper at Dewey Wong's wild restaurant on East Fifty-eighth Street as a way of apology. I gave him a little private hell, but it didn't take long to get back on our old footing. He was red-faced about it, but too much cop to let it bother him. What really had him going was the maximum effort order that was out in the department, recalling all officers from vacation, assigning extra working hours, canceling days off and hoping to keep the reason for the project secret long enough to get the job done. With the same thing going on all over the country, it wasn't going to be easy. Until it was finished, every other investigation was going to be at a standstill. When we finished, Eddie took off to start working on his end and I rode back downtown with Pat. In the car I said, "Velda told me about Lippy working the theater areas."

"I hope it satisfies you."

"Ahh . . ."

"Come on, Mike, stay loose. It's pretty damn obvious, isn't it?"

"There's still a killer around."

"More than one, buddy, and we're not concentrating any on your old pal. From now on we'll be going after the biggest and the best for one reason only . . . to give the papers all the hot news they can handle so maybe they'll skip over this latest incident. We're in trouble, Mike."

"Never changes. There's always trouble."

"And I don't need any with you."

I handed him the insurance papers and note Heidi had given me. He glanced at them and handed them back, his face masked with total astonishment. "By damn, you land right in the middle of the biggest mess we've ever had and all you want is a passkey to some broad's tail. Man, you never change! You damn horny . . ."

"Lay off, Pat. I could have had that for free yesterday."

"Then why . . ."

"It'll keep you off my back if for no other reason."

"For that I'll do anything. Look, take every one of those wallets and give them back personally. It won't be

48

hard to arrange at all. Then go get drunk or shack up for a week or get lost in the mountains . . . just anything at all!"

"My pleasure," I said.

He slammed his hand down on his knee with a disgusted gesture and shut up again. But he meant what he said. He packaged the whole lot for me, had me sign for each item and let me leave so he could handle all the traffic that was beginning to jam the room.

Outside, I set my watch with the clock in a jeweler's window. It was a quarter to eleven. The night was clear and an offshore breeze had blown the smog inland. You could see some of the stars that were able to shine through the reflected glow of the city lights. Traffic was thin downtown, but up farther New York would be coming to life. Or death, whichever way you looked at it. For me, I couldn't care less because it had always been that way anyway. At least the little episode with all the forces of national and international governments had bought me the same thing it had bought them . . . time. Everybody would be too busy to be clawing at my back now. I grinned silently and flagged down a cruising cab.

Finero's Steak House was jammed with the after-theater crowd, a noisy bunch three deep around the bar and a couple dozen others waiting patiently in the lobby for a table. I waved the maître d' over, told him all I wanted was to see Ballinger and he let the velvet rope down so I could go in.

He was like something out of a late-late movie, sitting there flanked by two full-blown blondes in dresses cut so low they seemed more like stage costumes than evening wear. His tux was the latest style, but on him it was all eyewash because he was still the dock-type hood and no tailor was ever going to change him. One of the blondes kept feeling his five o'clock shadow and murmuring about his virility. The other was doing something else and Ballinger was enjoying the mutual attention. The others respectfully ignored the play, paying due attention to their own dates. The original pair were there, but a new one had been added, a punk named Larry Beers who had been a *pistolero* with the Gomez Swan mob when he was nineteen and graduated into the upper echelon brackets when he had beaten a rap for gunning down two of the Benson Hill bunch. I didn't know Ballinger had him on his side until now. Old Woodring was paying high for his services, whatever they were, that was for sure.

This time Woody put on an act for everybody's benefit.

49

I got a big smile, an introduction to the girls whose names all sounded alike, the pair named Carl and Sammy, but when he came to Larry Beers I said, "We've met," His handshake was very wary. "Been a long time Larry."

"Let's make it longer the next time."

"Why not?"

Ballinger gave me a big smile that was all snake with the fangs out, his heavy-lidded eyes asking for trouble. "Join us, Hammer?"

"Not tonight, Woody. I got better things to do."

"Ah, come one, I'll get you a broad and . . ."

"I'm a leg man, myself," I said.

The blonde on his left stuck her tongue out at me. "I have those too, you know."

"I hope so. It's just that I enjoy a certain style and design."

She laughed and put both her hands on the table. Woody seemed annoyed at the sudden attention I was getting and let his smile fade. "You want something?"

I reached in my pocket, took out his wallet and tossed it on the table. "Just saving some embarrassment by having you go down and get it. Seems funny, an old pro like you letting a dip grab his poke. You do what I asked you?"

He was too happy to know I was leaving not to answer me. He stuck the wallet back in his pocket without looking at it and said, "Not yet, but soon."

"Real soon, okay?"

I looked at them all briefly, remembering their faces, nodded and went back to the street. I could feel Woody Ballinger's eyes boring into my back all the way.

On the way to the East Side I stopped in a gin mill on Sixth Avenue and put in a call to Velda at her apartment. I let the phone ring a dozen times, but there was no answer. I tried the office too in case she decided to work late. Same thing. The answering service for my apartment number told me there had been no calls for me at all. I wasn't about to worry about her. She had a P.I. ticket and a nasty little .32 hammerless automatic to go with it and when the chips were down she could take care of herself. Right now she probably was following orders, purse swinging with the come-on look in Lippy's neighborhood, seeing how the other half lived.

Near-midnight callers on actress tenants mustn't have seemed unusual to the doorman. He was the same one who had admitted me earlier and when I asked him if he ever slept he chuckled and said, "Changed shifts with

Barney. He's courting and the night work was ruining his love life. You want to see Miss Anders, go right up. She got in a little while ago and for her it's like the middle of the afternoon." He gave me a knowing look and added, "You want I should call her?"

"Give her a buzz. Hammer's the name."

"Yes, sir." He plugged in the jack, flipped the toggle twice and waited. Then: "Miss Anders, I have a Mr. Hammer . . ."

Her voice, ringing with that odd quality that could carry right through a phone, came right over his, but this time with a hurried urgency that seemed to have a catch in it. "Yes, please, send him right up."

The doorman hung up and made a wry face at me. "Funny broad, that."

"How come?"

"Any guy she can get, but always picks the wrong ones who give her a hard time. Like tonight she comes home, eyes all red, sniffling and jumpy. You'd think she'd blow this coop and start over somewheres."

"The mortality rate is pretty high in show business. Those dames can attract some oddballs."

"Yeah, but no reason to. They're just people same as anybody else. They got a face and a body and you'd think they'd make out okay, but this one is always miserable. It's a wonder she'll even speak to a guy any more. A big star, plenty of money and always down in the dumps. Me, I'm plain glad to be what I am."

"I know the feeling," I said.

This time I didn't have to touch the bell. The door was cracked and she was waiting for me, a pert thing with crazy ash-blonde hair, belted into a sheer black housecoat that clung so magically to all the curves and hollows that it seemed like she didn't have anything on at all.

But she wasn't quite as pretty as the last time. Her eyes were too red and feverish looking. The nervousness was more acute and the smile she gave me was strained to its limit. She swallowed with a tiny, jerky motion of her head and reached for my sleeve. "Come in, Mike. Please come in. I guess you must think I'm awfully strange to be having guests so late, but it's really nothing for me. Nothing at all." She tried a laugh on as she shut the door and took my hat. It had a hollow, flat sound. "You'll have to excuse me if I'm not at my best. It's just that . . . well, I imagine everyone has personal problems and . . ."

"Don't let it bother you, honey."

Heidi Anders' fingers squeezed hard on my arm and she

nibbled gently on her lower lip. Something like a shudder ran through her, then she tugged and let me feel the warmth of her body beside me as she took me into that nutty love nest of hers. Maybe it was the maid's day off, but the place wasn't like it had been. Too many things were out of place; cushions strewn around, a lamp on the floor, ashtrays filled with lipstick-smeared butts. They weren't party signs or trouble signs . . . just diffident neglect as if nobody gave a damn about the place.

She pushed me onto the couch, forcing gaiety into her tone. "Can I make you a drink, Mike?"

"A short one maybe. I can only stay a minute."

"Oh?" I couldn't tell whether it was fright or disappointment in her expression.

"I only came to bring your compact back." I reached in my pocket, took out the diamond-studded case and her insurance papers and laid them on the coffee table.

For all she seemed to care it could have been a piece of junk. She turned quickly, called back, "Thank you. It was very kind," over her shoulder, and went to the small mahogany bar in the corner and made me a drink. She came back and handed it to me. The ice in the glass clinked against the sides and she put it down quickly so I wouldn't notice her hand tremble.

I said, "None for you?"

"No . . . not now." She pulled a tissue from one slash pocket and touched her nose and eyes with it, the corners of her mouth crinkling in a smile. "I guess I shouldn't be so sentimental over small things," she said. "You'll have to excuse me." She reached for the compact and the insurance policy. "Maybe I'd better put·these where they won't get lost again. Be right back."

I nodded and tasted my drink. She had made it too strong, but it was still good. She disappeared into her bedroom and closed the door behind her. I took another sip of my drink and got up and walked around the room, studying the decorations. There were framed photos of Heidi in her lavish stage costumes, others deliberately posed, provocative bikini scenes taken against white sand and palm tree backgrounds. Some were ornaments that could have been taken for the ruins of Pompeii. The oil paintings were original and unique, all with a carefully guarded sexual motif. The pieces that were obviously foreign were rare and expensive, half of them reflecting the phallic theme, but the other half a little out of place since they were the result of good and expensive taste.

Too bad there weren't more of them. I finished my drink and put the glass back on the bar.

I started back to the couch when Heidi said, "Sorry I took so long. I had to freshen up."

When I turned around I felt my mouth go dry and the muscles tightened across my shoulders. It was Heidi, all right, but the curtain had gone up and it was another Heidi altogether. The fever in her eyes had turned into a deep sultry azure. The smile was real, tantalizing, and when she walked toward me the sway was there, the slow, female gesticulations with the hips and thighs that could make them all so damn sure of themselves because they knew what it could do to a man. She had rearranged the housecoat so that the lapels were thrown open to the shoulders, the translucent fabric passing over breasts only half covered, to the belt at her waist. Her eyes held mine, letting me take her all in, then she stopped in a deliberate pose and the rest of the housecoat parted so that I could see all of her at once. Luscious, firm, silken, with the lightest of tans that offset hair that was tousled and ash-blonde, *and not tousled and not ash-blonde*.

The tableau was only momentary before she came to me and took my hand. This time hers wasn't shaking at all. I turned her around, put my fingers under the chin and tilted her head up to me. Very slowly, her tongue licked her lips, making them glisten softly, her eyes intense and sleepy looking. But I didn't kiss her. I let my fingertips run under her sleeves, caressing her skin gently, then I led her to the couch and eased her down. She quivered gently and smiled, squirming into the soft cushions, her eyes still sleepy and hungry.

"I'll be right back," I said and she nodded dreamily.

I went into the bedroom and it only took me two minutes to find the compact and another one to locate the catch that let the back of it drop open. It was made to hold another type of powdered cosmetic, and what was there was a powder, all right, but it wasn't cosmetic. The syringe was in a velvet case in her large jewel box. I took them both back to the living room and walked to the couch.

Heidi was lying there waiting. She had opened the belt and thrown the housecoat wide open. One hand half cupped a breast and her thighs were parted in invitation. Her eyes were closed but the one in the center of her belly was watching me avidly.

I said, "Heidi," her eyes came open and she smiled. "You're a junkie."

Then her eyes went wide and the smile stopped.

"No wonder you needed that compact so badly, kid. Who cut off your supply?"

No vibrancy in her voice now at all. Nothing but sheer childish fear, weak and hesitant. "Mike . . ."

"You're a great actress, kid. You faked it nicely, but then, you didn't have much of a choice. A real loud beef about the loss might have brought in a smart insurance investigator who would have found your stash, or a trip to the police lost-and-found meant taking a chance talking to a wised-up cop who spotted your symptoms and got the picture right away."

"Please, Mike . . ."

"You're lucky, doll." I tossed the compact down on the table. "It's your problem, not mine, and I'm not making it mine. I could dump this stuff but you'd only find another supplier. I could turn you in but some sweet judge would only turn you out again, especially if it were your first rap. The resulting publicity could kill you altogether or could make you bigger than ever. That's happened too. All I want to tell you is that you're a jerk. The complete clown. A raggedy-ass damn fool idiot and right now you're able to know what I'm talking about. You're probably not on too bad, but you're hooked and you're scared to bust it. All you can do is go downhill and lose everything you ever worked for and pretty soon you'll be working even harder peddling your behind ten times a day for enough to buy a jolt. You look great lying there right now and if you were for real I'd join the fun and games and come away with a great memory, but you're not for real any more and I wouldn't waste my time at it. So give it a big thought, baby, if you're capable of it. Think about it every day and do what you please. You can come back to the land of the living or start getting all your papers and photos in order so that when they find your lovely little corpse in the river or on the floor with a deliberate overdose because it all got too much for you, the newshounds will be able to give you a nice, lurid send-off in the obit columns."

She had never stopped watching me. Those azure eyes were wide open, unconsciously wet. One hand pulled the front of the housecoat across the slow heave of her stomach and her breasts moved with a quick intake of breath.

I got my hat from the table beside the door and got the hell out of there. I walked eight blocks toward my apartment before I bothered to flag down a cab. When I got home I showered, had another drink and flopped down on the bed, looking at nothing on the ceiling.

Stupid, idiotic broad. But I was just as sore at myself. Something about the whole deal should have told me something and I was too aggravated to put it in its right place.

CHAPTER 5

By noontime I had reduced Lippy's haul to two undelivered wallets. The owner of the rather shabby job lived and worked in Queens and made an appointment to meet me at my office on Saturday to pick it up. The other belonged to William Dorn who was about to donate to the P.A.L. like the others. A maid gave me his office number and when I called him he was appreciative and invited me to lunch at The Chimes, a sedate and expensive restaurant on East Fifty-seventh Street. My taste didn't run to exotic French cuisine, but the change could be different and I made a one o'clock date to see him there. I tried another call to the office and Velda's apartment but she was at neither place so I rang Eddie Dandy and he was glad to take a beer break with me for a half hour.

I had to laugh when I saw him. It wasn't the hell he had caught from the network for making waves or the embarrassment of sweating out the snide remarks from the rest of the staff. It was the agony of having to sit on a story he knew was hot and not being able to release it.

He downed a tall schooner of lager without stopping, belched once and called for another. "Only one thing got me, buddy. Suppose somebody else pieces it together the same way I did."

"Quit worrying. By now they have it all nicely organized with everybody briefed properly and they'll be able to con the best cynic into taking their word for it. Right now it's a dead issue."

"Not to a couple of guys I know. They couldn't picture me doing an about-face like that. You catch my retraction?"

"Missed it."

"That's the trouble with color TV. They could see the egg all over my face in bright yellow against screaming red. It wasn't easy, pal. I hope when I make the next announcement I'm not a pasty white. If they don't get that stuff this whole country could be wiped out. You know anything about the germ warfare developments?"

"Just what I read in the papers."

"Well, it isn't pretty and you're not going to be reading much about it at all. That stuff is as top secret as it can get. Right now they're flooding us with news stories from every direction you can think of just to keep the public's mind off my big squeal. It may work and it may not. We've had the switchboard lit up like a star burst since I broke it and have operators working overtime with nice pat explanations. They're even sending form letters out to those who want them. It's rough, boy, rough. What are you up to?"

"Some simple legwork on a simple matter," I said.

"You still on that Sullivan deal?"

I nodded.

"A lost cause, Mike. They pull the cops in to track down Schneider's killers, they schedule a special political parade to cover the vacation wipe-out, the Crime Commission is laying it on heavy and you couldn't bust a cop loose for special detail work for anything. Nope, you won't get any leg up from the cops until this is over."

"I'm not asking for any."

"Okay, you know the story. You're making a federal case out of a simple murder and robbery. Why?"

"Beats me" I told him. "Maybe because I believed something nobody else believed."

"Hell, people will believe anything. Look what happened with me."

"So waste time. So feel lousy. What's left to do?"

I told him about the wallets and my date with Dorn. I didn't mention Heidi Anders at all.

"William Dorn?" he asked.

"Know him?"

"Park Avenue offices?"

"That's the one."

"Sure, he's chairman of the board of Anco Electronics, his March Chemical Company engineered that new oil refining process the industry has turned to and now he's gone heavy in mining. You're traveling in fancy company, kiddo. I never thought I'd see the day. Ole Mike Hammer, denizen of the side streets, partying with café society. Better not let it get to be a habit."

I looked at my watch. "Well, if it does, it starts now." I finished my beer, flipped Eddie for the drinks, won the toss and told him so long. At one o'clock on the nose I walked into The Chimes, got a disapproving stare from the maître d' until I asked for Mr. Dorn's table, then his professional subservient attitude returned with a fawning nod and he bowed me to a table in a hand-carved, oak-paneled booth on the dais-like section of the main room that was obviously reserved for only the most select clientele.

Most actors would like to age into a man like William Dorn. A few have, but only a few. He was tall and lean with a tanned, rugged face and intelligent eyes under a thick shock of wavy hair streaked with gray. When I took his hand he had a strong, sure grip and I knew he wasn't as lean as he looked. Suddenly I felt like a slob. He was one of those guys who could look good in anything and I knew why the amused woman, with the hair so raven black it was darker than the shadows she sat in, could be so much at ease with him.

"Mr. Hammer," he said in a pleasantly deep voice, "William Dorn, and may I present Miss Renée Talmage."

She had held out her hand and I took it gently. "A pleasure," I said.

"Very nice to see you, Mr. Hammer." Her smile broke around a set of even gleaming white teeth and she added, "Please sit down."

"Miss Talmage is head of accounting at Anco. Have you heard of us?"

"Just this afternoon."

"Don't let it bother you, Mr. Hammer. Our business is not one that goes in heavily for publicity and promotion. Care for a drink before lunch?"

"Rye and ginger'll do," I said.

The waiter hovering behind me took the order and disappeared. I pulled Dorn's wallet from my pocket and handed it to him. He took it, flipped it open and scanned his credit cards and held it up to show Renée Talmage. "Now that is efficient police work. Imagine."

"Strictly accidental, Mr. Dorn." I pushed a receipt and my pen across to him. "Mind signing for it?"

"Not at all." He scrawled a signature in the proper place and I folded the receipt back into my pocket.

He said, "In a way, it's a shame to put you to all the trouble. I've already canceled the credit cards, but my driver's license and club cards are really the valuable items."

"Sorry you didn't get your money back too. It rarely happens, though, so feel lucky you even got anything."

"Yes, I do. Very. There's a matter of a reward that I mentioned."

"A check to the Police Athletic League will do nicely, Mr. Dorn."

For the first time Renée Talmage leaned out of the shadows. She was even lovelier than I had taken her to be. I figured her age in the early thirties when a woman was at her best, but it was almost impossible to pin it down accurately. "Mr. Hammer ... your name is very familiar."

I had to give her a silly grin. "Yeah, I know."

"Are you ..."

I didn't let her go any further. "Yeah, I'm the one," I said.

Dorn let out a little laugh and gave us both a quizzical look. "Now what is this all about? Trust Renée here to come up with something odd about even the most complete stranger."

"What she means, Mr. Dorn, is that I'm not with the police department at all. I'm a licensed private investigator who gets into enough trouble to make enough headlines to be recognized on occasions, which, funny enough, is good for business but hell on the hide occasionally. It was a guy I once knew who had your wallet among others. I located them and I'm paying my last respects by getting them back where they came from."

Dorn recognized the seriousness in my voice and nodded. "I understand. Quite long ago ... I had to do something similar. And this person you knew?"

"Dead now."

The drinks came then and we raised our glasses to each other, two Manhattans against a highball, tasted them and nodded our satisfaction and put them down. Renée Talmage was still looking at me and Dorn gave me another chuckle. "I'm afraid you're in for it now. My bloodthirsty co-worker here is an avid follower of mysteries in literature and films. She'll press you for every detail if you let her." He reached over and laid his hand on her arm. "Please, dear. The man was a friend of Mr. Hammer."

"It doesn't matter," I said. "I have more than one friend with an illegal pastime. Too bad it caught up with him. So far it's tabbed as murder that came out of an attempted robbery."

"Attempted?" Renée Talmage leaned forward, the interest plain on her face.

"They never got what they went after. The money was all banked, squirreled away in a neighborhood account."

"But the wallets . . ."

"Discarded," I told her. "With a guy like him it would be too chancy to risk using credit cards. He just wasn't the type to own one."

"And that's your story," Dorn said to her. "I think we can talk about more pleasant things while we eat."

"Spoilsport," she grimaced. "At last I have a chance to talk to a real private cop and you ruin it." She looked at me, eyes twinkling. "Look out, Mr. Hammer, I may deliberately cultivate you, regardless."

"Then start by calling me Mike. This Mr. Hammer routine gives me the squirms."

Her laugh was rich and warm. "I was hoping you'd ask. So then, I am Renée, but this is William."

Dorn looked at me sheepishly. "Unfortunately, I never acquired a nickname. Oh, I tried, but I guess I'm just the William type. Odd, don't you think?"

"I don't know. Look at the trouble our last Vice President had. He had to settle for initials. At least you look like the *mister* belongs there."

We ordered then, something in French that turned out to be better than I expected, and between courses Dorn drifted into his business. He had started out during the war years assembling radar components under military contract, developed a few patentable ideas and went on from there. He admitted freely that World War II, Korea and the Vietnam thing made him wealthy, but didn't hesitate to state that the civilian applications of his products were of far more benefit than could be accrued by the military. Hell, I didn't disagree with him. You make it whenever and however you can. Separate ethics from business and you get a big fat nothing.

Apparently Renée Talmage had been with him for ten years or so and was a pretty valuable asset to his business. Several times she came up with items of interest that belonged more in a man's world than a woman's. Dorn saw my look of surprise and said, "Don't mind the brainy one, Mike. She does that to me sometimes . . . the big answers from those pretty lips. I pay her handsomely for her insight and she hasn't been wrong yet. My only concern is that she might leave me and go in business for herself. That would be the end of my enterprises."

"I can imagine. I got one like that myself," I said.

At two thirty I told them I had to split, waited while Dorn signed the tab and walked to the street with them. Someplace the sun had disappeared into the haze and a bank of heavy, low clouds was beginning to roll in again. I offered to drop them off, but Dorn said they were going to walk back and gave me another firm handshake.

When Renée held out her fingers to me her eyes had that sparkle in them again and she said, "I really *am* going to cultivate you, Mike. I'm going to get you alone for lunch and make you tell me everything about yourself."

"That won't be hard," I said.

Dorn had turned away to say hello to a foursome that followed us out and never heard her soft, impish answer. "It will be, Mike."

I got back to the office and picked up the mail that had been shoved through the slot in the door and tossed it on Velda's desk. For five minutes I prowled around, wondering why the hell she didn't call, then went back to the mail again. There were bills, four checks, a couple of circulars and something I damned near missed, a yellow envelope from the messenger service we sometimes used. I ripped it open and dumped out the folded sheet inside.

The handwriting was hers, all right. All it said was *"Call Sammy Brent about theater tickets. Will call office tonight."* The envelope was dated one fifteen, delivered from the Forty-fifth Street messenger service office. Whatever she was getting at was beyond me. Sammy Brent ran a tiny ticket office dealing mainly in off-Broadway productions and dinner theaters in the New York-New Jersey-Connecticut area.

The Yellow Pages listed his agency and I dialed the number, getting a heavy, lower East Side accent in an impatient hello twice. I said, "Sammy?"

"Sure, who else? You think I can afford help here?"

"Mike Hammer, buddy."

"Hey, Mike, whattaya know?"

"Velda said I should call you about theater tickets. What the hell's going on?"

"Yeah, yeah. That crazy broad of yours shows up here like some Times Square floozie on the loose and I didn't even know her. Man, what legs! She's got her dress up to ... good thing the old lady wasn't around. Man, she's got a top and bottom you can't ..."

"What's with the tickets?"

"Oh." His voice suddenly went quiet. "Well, she was asking about Lippy Sullivan. Real sorry about that, Mike."

"I know."

"Good guy, him. You know, he was hustlin' for me."

"What?"

"He picked up extra change scalping tickets. Not for the big shows, but like the regular ones I handle. Conventions come in, those guys got a broad and no place to go, he'd meet them in bars and hotels and hustle tickets."

"What!"

"He was a good guy, Mike."

"Look, how'd you pay him?"

"Cash. He'd get a percent of the price over the going rate. Like maybe a buck or two. It was a good deal. We was both satisfied. You know, he was a good talker. He could make friends real easy. That's why he did pretty good at it. No fortune, but he picked up walking-around money." When I didn't answer him he said, "It was okay, wasn't it, Mike? Like I ain't the only one who . . . "

"It was okay, Sammy. Thanks."

And it was starting to spell out a brand-new story.

I searched my memory for the return address that had been on the envelope in Lippy's garbage, finally remembered it as being simply NEW USED FURNITURE on Eighth Avenue and dug the number out of the directory.

Yes, the clerk remembered Lippy buying a couch. It wasn't often they sold a new one in that neighborhood. He had picked it out on a Saturday afternoon just a couple of weeks before he died and paid for it in cash with small bills. No, he didn't say why he wanted it. But permament roomers in the area often changed furniture. The landlords wouldn't and what transients usually rented with their meager earnings were hardly worth using. I thanked the clerk and hung up.

When I looked down the .45 was in my hand, the butt a familiar thing against my palm. It was black and oily with walnut grips, an old friend who had been down the road with me a long time.

I slid it back in the holster and walked to the window so I could look out at the big city of fun. The clouds were rolling around the edges, melting into each other, bringing a premature darkness down around the towering columns of brick and steel. It's a big place, New York. Millions of people who run down holes in the ground like moles, or climb up the sides of cliffs to their own little caves. Most were just people. Just plain people. And then there were the others, the killers. There was one out there now and that one belonged all to me.

Okay, Lippy, the pattern's showing its weave now. Sammy nailed it down without knowing it. You worked your tail off for an honest buck but you were just too damn friendly. Who did you meet, Lippy? What dip hustling the

*theater district did you pick up to move in with you?
Sure, I could understand it. Dames were out of your
line. It was strictly friends and how many did you have?
You were glad to have somebody get close to you, to yak
with and drink with. You found a friend, Lippy, until you
found out he wasn't honest like you were. You latched onto
a lousy cheap crook. What happened, pal? Maybe you
located his cache and stuck it where he couldn't get to it,
then dumped those wallets in the garbage. So he came
back and tried to take it from you. No, Lippy, there
wasn't any reason at all for it, was there? You would
have shared your pad, your income, your beer ... anything to keep him straight and your friend that you could
believe in and trust. No reason for him to kill you at all.
Only I have a reason, friend, and my reason is bigger than
the one you didn't have.*

All I had to do was find the right pickpocket.

So I sat there and ran it over in my mind until I could
see it happen. It shouldn't be too much of a job now I
knew in which direction to take off. There was only that
little nagging thought that something was out of focus.
Something I should see clearly. It wasn't that complicated
at all.

Outside, the darkness had sucked the daylight out of the
city and I sat there watching it fight back with bravely lit
windows in empty offices and the weaving beams of head-
lights from the street traffic. In a little while the flow
would start from the restaurants to the theaters and it
would be the working hour for the one I wanted. If he
was there.

Meyer Solomon was a bailbondsman who owed me a
favor and he was glad to pay it back. I asked him to find
out if anybody had been booked on a pickpocket charge
within the last two days and he told me he'd check it out
right away. So I stayed by the phone for another forty
minutes until it finally jangled and I picked it up.

"Mike? Meyer here."

"Let's have it."

"Got six of 'em. Four were bums working the subway
on sleepers and the other two are pros. You looking to
hire one of 'em?"

"Not quite. Who are the pros?"

"Remember Coo-Coo Weist?"

"Damn, Meyer, he must be eighty years old."

"Still working, though. Made a mistake when he tried it
on an off-duty detective."

"Who else?"

"A kid named Johnny Baines. A Philly punk who came here about three years ago. Good nimble fingers on that guy. The last time he was busted he was carrying over ten grand. This time he only had a couple hundred on him but it wasn't his fault."

"Why not?"

Meyer let out a sour laugh. "Because he was only three hours out of the clink where he spent ninety days on a D and D rap. He never really had a chance to get operating right. You going bail for somebody, Mike?"

"Not this time, Meyer. Thanks."

"Anytime, Mike."

I hung up and went back to the window again.

He was still out there somewhere.

I called downstairs, had a sandwich, coffee and the evening papers sent up. The hunt was getting heavier for Schneider's killers and the reporters were hitting every detail with relish. Another time it would have been funny, because contract killers who blasted one of their own kind seldom got that kind of attention. Right now they'd be running scared, not only from the cops, but from the guy who gave them the job. Their business days were over. Two National Guard units were being called out on a security maneuver, detailed upstate. The same thing was happening in five other states. In view of the tense international situation the military deemed it smart policy to stay prepared. It made for lots of space, dozens of pictures and if somebody was lucky they might come up with something. Somehow I didn't feel very excited about sitting on the edge of annihilation.

At twelve fifteen the phone went off beside my ear and I rolled off the old leather couch and grabbed it. My voice still sounded husky from being asleep and I said, "Yeah?"

"Mike?" Her voice sounded guarded.

"Where the hell have you been, Velda?"

"Shut up and listen. I rented one of those fleabag apartments across the street from Lippy's rooming house, downstairs in the front. If you called Sammy Brent then you have it spotted . . . the tickets and all?"

"Loud and clear. Lippy had somebody staying with him."

"That's what it looks like, but he was never seen going in or out and nobody seems to know a thing about it. Apparently he was a pretty cagy character to get away with that, but I know how he did it. In this neighborhood at the right hours he wouldn't be noticed at all."

"All right kid, get with it."

"Somebody's in Lippy's old room right now. I spotted the beam of a pencil flash under the window shade."

"Damn!"

"I can move in . . ."

"You stay put, you hear? I'll be there in ten minutes."

"That can be too late."

"Let it. Just watch for me. I'll get off at the corner and walk on up. Cover the outside and keep your ass down."

I grabbed an extra clip for the .45 out of the desk drawer, slammed the door shut behind me and used the stairs instead of waiting for the elevator. A cab was ahead of me, waiting for a red light at the corner and I reached it as the signals changed and told him where to go. When the driver saw the five I threw on the seat beside him he made it across town and south to the corner I wanted in exactly six minutes and didn't bother to stick around to see what it was all about.

It was an old block, a hangover from a century of an orgy of progress, a four-storied chasm with feeble yellow eyes to show that there still was a pulse beat somewhere behind the crumbling brownstone facades. Halfway down the street a handful of kids were playing craps under an overhead light and on the other side a pair of drifters were shuffling toward Ninth. It wasn't the kind of street you bothered to sit around and watch at night. It was one you wanted to get away from.

I flashed a quick look at the rooftops and the areaways under the stoops when I reached Lippy's old place, found nothing and spotted Velda in the doorway across the street. I gave her the "wait and see" signal, then took the sandstone steps two at a time, the .45 in my hand.

A 25-watt bulb hung from a dropcord in the ceiling of the vestibule and I reached up and unscrewed it, making sure I had my distance and direction to the right door clear in my mind. The darkness would have been complete except for the pale glow that seeped out from under the super's door, but it was enough. His TV was on loud enough to cover any sound my feet might make and I went past his apartment to Lippy's and tried the knob.

The door was locked.

I took one step back, planted myself and thumbed the hammer back on the rod. Then I took a running hop, smashed the door open with my foot and went rolling inside taking furniture with me that was briefly outlined in the white blast of a gunshot that sent a slug ripping into the floor beside my head.

My hand tightened on the butt of the .45 and blew the

darkness apart while I was skittering in a different direction, the wild thunder of the shot echoing around the room. Glass crashed from the far end and a chair went over, then running legs hit me when I was halfway up, fell and I had my hands on his neck, wrenched him back and banged two fast rights into his ear and heard him let out a choked yell. Whoever he was, he was big and strong and wrenched out of my hands, his arms flailing. I swung with the gun, felt the sight rip into flesh and skull bone. It was almost enough and I would have had him the next time around, but the beam of a pencil flash hit me in the face and there was a dull, clicking sound against the top of my head and all the strength went out of me in one full gush.

A faraway voice said almost indistinctly, "Get up so I can kill him!" But then there were two popping sounds, a muffled curse, and I lay there in the dreary state of semiconsciousness knowing something was happening without knowing or caring what until a hazy dawn of artificial light made everything finally come into misty focus that solidified into specific little objects I could recognize.

Velda said, "You stupid jerk."

"Don't be redundant," I told her. "Where are they?"

"Out. Gone. The back window was open for a secondary exit and they used it. If I hadn't fired coming into the building you would have been dead by now."

The yelling and screaming of the fun watchers on the street were coming closer and a siren was whining to a stop in front of the house. I pushed myself to a sitting position, saw the .45 on the floor and reached for it. I thumbed out the clip, ejected the live slug in the breech, caught it and slid it back into the clip, then reloaded the piece and stuck it back in the holster. "You see them?" I asked.

"No."

I took a quick look around the room before they all came in. The place was a shambles. Even the paper had been torn off the walls. "Somebody else figured it out too," I said.

"What were they after, Mike?"

"Something pretty easily hidden," I told her.

CHAPTER 6

Pat came in while they were taking my statement, listened impassively as I detailed the events at Lippy's place and when I signed the sheets, walked over and threw a leg over the edge of the desk. "You can't keep your nose clean, can you?"

"You ought to be happy about extra diversions from what I hear," I said.

"Not your kind." Pat glanced sidewise at Velda. "Why didn't you call for a squad car?"

Velda threw him an amused smile. "I wanted to be subtle about it. Besides, I wouldn't want to get fired."

I said, "Why the beef, Pat? We interrupted a simple break-in and attempted robbery."

"Like hell you did."

"Nothing illegal about it. Any citizen could pull it off."

"You managed to goof," he reminded me. "They got away."

"They didn't get what they were after."

"What *were* they after, Mike?"

I gave a meaningless shrug.

Pat picked up a pencil and twirled it in his fingers. "Let's have it, Mike," he said softly.

"Lippy was right, Pat. He got killed for no reason at all. He was a hardworking slob who made friends with some dip working the area and took him into the rooming house with him. That's the one they were after."

Pat's eyes half closed, watching me closely. "Something was in one of those wallets ..."

"Maybe not," I said. "Apparently the guy was with Lippy a few weeks before Lippy got onto him and booted him out. That bunch of wallets was probably just his last day's take. You know who they all belonged to."

"And one guy was Woody Ballinger."

"Yeah, I know."

"Keep talking," Pat said.

67

"How many good pickpockets do you know who never took a fall?"

"They all do sooner or later."

"None of the prints you picked up from the apartment got any action, did they?"

Pat's lips twisted in a grin. "You're guessing, but you're right. The set we sent to Washington turned out negative. No record of them anywhere, not even military."

"That gives us one lead then," I said. "Most people stay within their own age groups, so he was a 4-F in his late forties."

"Great," Pat said.

"And without a record, maybe he wasn't a regular practicing dip at all. Somebody could have been after him for what he did before he took up the profession."

"That still leaves us with nothing."

"Oh, we have something, all right," I said.

"Like what?" Pat asked me.

"Like what they didn't get yet. They'll keep looking."

The other two cops and the steno collected their papers, nodded to Pat and left the three of us alone in the room. Pat swung off the desk in that lazy way he had and stared out the window. Finally he said, "We haven't got time to throw any manpower into this right now." There was something tight in his voice. I felt Velda's eyes on me, but didn't react.

"I know."

"You be damn careful, Mike. My neck's out now too."

"No sweat." I lit a cigarette and tossed the match in the wastebasket. "Any progress yet?"

He didn't look at me. "No."

"The lid on pretty tight?"

"Nothing will ever be tighter." He took a deep breath and turned around. In the backlight from the window his face looked drawn. "If you turn up anything, keep in touch. We still have a primary job to do."

"Sure, Pat."

I picked up my hat and reached for Velda's arm. I knew the question was on her lips, but she said nothing except for a so long to Pat. When we got down on the street to hunt up a cab she asked evenly, "What was that all about?"

It was a nice night for New York. The wind had cleaned the smog out of the skies and you could see the stars. Kids walked by holding hands, traffic was idling along and behind the lighted windows families would be watching the late news. Only nobody was telling them that

68

the biggest news of all they wouldn't want to hear. They were all living in wonderful ignorance, not knowing that they might be living their last night. For one second I wished I was in the same boat as they were.

I took Velda's hand and started across the street to intercept a cab going north. "Just some departmental business," I said. "Nothing important."

But she knew I was lying. There was a sadness in the small smile she gave me and her hand was flaccid in mine. Keeping details from Velda wasn't something I was used to doing. Not too long ago she had taken a pair of killers off my back without a second's hesitation. Now she was thinking that I couldn't trust her.

I said, "Later, kitten. Believe me, I have a damn good reason."

Her hand snuggled back into mine again and I knew it was all right. "What do you want me to do now?" Velda asked.

"Back on the trail. I want that dip. He could still be in the area."

"Even if he knew somebody was out to kill him?"

"There's no better place to hide than right here in the city. If he's any kind of a pro he's been working. If he's moved in on somebody else's turf they'll be the first to dump him. So make your contacts and buy what you have to. Just lay off any hard action. I'll take care of that end."

"How do we clear any messages?"

"Let's use the office. I'll keep the tape recorder on and we can bleep in any cross information." Both of us carried electronic units that could activate the tape in either direction so it wasn't necessary to have someone in the office all the time.

"Where are you going to be, Mike?"

"Seeing what an old enemy is up to."

"Woody Ballinger?"

"Uh-huh."

"He can't afford to lose any more," Velda said.

"Neither can I, sugar," I said.

"What brings you back to him again?"

All I could think of was Heidi Anders' compact. What she had in it put her life on the line. I said, "Somebody's not after money. Woody used to keep all his business in his head. Maybe he put some of it in his wallet this time. A smart dip could have spotted it and tried a little blackmail."

But first I had to be sure.

69

They wouldn't talk to the cops. To a uniform or a badge they were deaf, dumb and blind, but I wasn't department material and they could read it in my face. I was one of them, living on the perimeter of normalcy and the ax I was grinding was a personal one because Lippy had been my friend and they had tried to knock me off too.

The redheaded whore called Skippy who had her crib across the back court from Lippy had seen them come out the window, two guys in dark suits she could tell didn't come from the neighborhood. They had jumped the fence and gone through the alley between her place and the dry cleaner's. No, she didn't see their faces, but the light hit one and she knew he was partially bald, but not too old because he could run too fast. She took the twenty I gave her since the excitement scared off the john she had in the pad and it was too late to turn another trick.

Old lady Gostovich had seen them go right past her when she was coming in from her nightly bash at the gin mill, but her eyes were bad and she was too bagged to make out their faces. All she could tell me was that they were in dark suits, climbed into a car and drove away. When she crunched the bill I handed her in her fist she added one more thing.

Between wheezes she said, "One wore them heel things."

"What heel things?"

"Clickers."

"Clickers?"

"Clickers. Like kids got, y'know?"

"No, I don't."

"Sheee-it, boy. They drag 'em over the floor and scratch everything up. Like dancers got on their shoes, y'know?"

"Metal taps?"

"So I call 'em clickers. Only on his heels. Maybe I don't see so good no more, but I hear. Boy, I hear everything. I even hear the cat pissin'. Thanks for the scratch." She looked down at the bill in her hand. "How much is it?"

"Ten bucks."

"Maybe I'll buy glasses." She looked up and gave me a gummy smile.

I said, "How many?"

"Enough to get slopped. Makes me feel young again, y'know?" She spit on the sidewalk and hunched her shabby coat around her shoulders, her eyes peering at me. "Sure, *you* know. Boy like you knows too damn much."

When she had shuffled off I started toward the corner, then stopped midblock to watch a convoy of Army trucks

70

rumble by, escorted by a pair of prowl cars with their flashers on, each giving a low growl of their sirens at the intersections as they went through the red lights. There were four jeeps and thirty-eight trucks, each filled with suddenly activated and annoyed-looking National Guardsmen. It hadn't been since the summer encampments that the city had seen one of these processions. I was wondering what excuse they were going to give the public if the public bothered to ask.

Overhead a cool northeast wind suddenly whistled through the TV antennaes on the rooftops and swirled down into the street, picking up dust and papers along the curbs and skittering them along the sidewalks. *Hell*, I thought, *it's going to rain again. Maybe it's better that way. People don't like to come out in the rain and if they don't they can't ask questions.*

Someplace Velda was roaming around the area doing the same thing I was doing only from a different direction and she could do it just as fast. And right now time was our enemy.

I shoved the bar door open and inched past the uglies with their serapes, the virgin-hair muttonchops and shoulder-length curls. They were the boys. The girls weren't any better. They smelled better, except the smell was artificial and I wondered if it were to enhance the little they had or cover up what they lacked. One idiot almost started to lip me until I squeezed his arm a little bit, then he whited out and let me go by with a sick grin his old man should have seen if he had chopped him in the mouth ten years ago when there was still hope for him.

Velda had called to say she had canvassed the neighborhood with no results so she was going back into the barnacle she had rented and keep a watch on Lippy's old apartment.

The other call was from Renée Talmage. "Mr. Tape Recorder," she said, "please tell Mr. Hammer that I am going to be waiting ever so impatiently for him in Dewey Wong's restaurant on Fifty-eighth Street, snuggled against the wall close to the window where all those lovely men will know I'm waiting for someone and perhaps not try to pick me up. And Mr. Tape Recorder, tell him that Dewey says he will stay open very late just to make sure Mr. Hammer gets here."

I hung up and looked at my watch. It was one twenty-five. Outside the phone booth the uglies were making time with the idiots. In New York, the uglies are the long-haired idiot guys. The idiots are the short-haired ugly

71

girls. It isn't easy to tell one from the other. One ugly didn't realize it, but he was kissing another ugly. In a way he was lucky. The idiot he was with was even uglier.

So I said the hell with it and grabbed a cab up to Dewey Wong's and got around the corner of the bar, sat down next to her and told beautiful Janie who was filling in for her old man behind the bar to bring me a rye and ginger.

"Pretty isn't she?" Renée asked.

"A mouth waiting to be kissed," I said.

"Dewey seems pretty capable."

"Ever since he's been colonialized," I told her.

"Colonialize me," Renée said. A little half laugh played around her mouth and her eyes were full of sparkles.

"Now?"

She lifted her glass in a challenge, the big black pupils inside all those gold flecks watching me closely. Carelessly, she said, "Why not?"

I let my hand run up the bare leg that was crossed over the other one until my fingers had the top of her bikini pants under their tips and said, "Ready?"

Her glass went back to the bar top very slowly, every movement deliberate and slow to make sure nobody was watching. Even the smile was unsure of itself. "You're crazy, Mike."

"I could have told you that."

"Take your hand out of my pants."

"I'm not done yet," I said. I took a drink of my highball. Janie grinned and turned away to serve another customer. At least she knew what was happening.

Almost pathetically, Renée said, "Please?"

"You wanted to be colonialized," I told her.

"But not in front of all these people."

"Tough," I said. She felt my fingers curling around that silly little hem they build into bikini pants. I wondered what color they were.

"I know a better place to find out," Renée told me.

I'm an old soldier. I grew up watching Georgia Sothern, Gypsy Rose Lee, Ann Corio and the rest on the stage of the old Apollo and Eltinge theaters and got my lessons in basic female anatomy from the best of them. There's never been a shape or size I couldn't slam into one category or another no matter what part I was looking at and get clinical about it at the same time. Women are women. The female counterpart. They're supposed to be something special, intelligent, loving, pneumatic, sexy as hell, incredibly beautiful, with that little thing they're instinctively supposed to do that can make a man turn inside out. Hardly any fit the pattern. Oh, I knew some.

Now I knew another.

She just stood there in the middle of the room and let the funny little smile do the teasing while she unzipped slowly and let the dress fall in a heap around her feet.

"Better?" Renée asked.

I nodded. But casually, because she still hadn't caught up to Georgia Sothern. That one could *really* take off her clothes. She used to do it to "Hold That Tiger," but that music would sound silly these days. "You're doing fine," I told her.

"Can I have a drink?"

I tasted my own highball and loosened my tie. "If that's what you need to uninhibit yourself, baby, the bar's right behind you."

She lifted herself on tiptoe, nothing on but a flesh-colored bra and bikini pants with other colors dominating the sheer mesh, and grinned at me like she was running all the plays. "Like?"

"I like," I said.

She hooked her thumb in the top of those bikini pants and pulled them down a bare inch. A little tumble of dark hair spilled out over the top. "Like?" Her voice was provocatively inquisitive.

"I like," I said again.

She took off her bra. She spilled out there too, full and high, heavy breasted with round, square-tipped, demanding nipples emerging from their even darker cores.

"Still like?" she asked. I watched her eyes drift down me, all stretched out on my own damn couch. For a second she was puzzled.

I said, "I'm a leg man, kid."

Then she grinned again and took off those flesh-colored bikini pants.

Naked women are pretty. Damn, but they're pretty. Any size, any shape you look, and when they're built like all those pinups we used to have on the inside of locker doors and the kind they plaster up in garages to keep your mind off the repair bills, they can con you into anything.

And Renée knew what I was thinking. "For real?" she asked.

"You must be one hell of a business asset," I said.

"William never saw me like this."

"Why not?"

73

She twirled around, picked the drinks off the bar and handed me another one. "He never put his hands inside my pants," she said.

"Stop being vulgar," I told her.

"Ho . . . yeah. Keep talking, fingers."

"I barely touched you."

"Except in the right spot," Renée said.

"Sorry about that."

"Yes, you are. Little scarred feathers extending from your wrist, delicate, woman-killing tentacles that touch and excite. Look at me, totally bare and throwing it at you, and you lying there with a drink in your hand and all you have off is your top collar button because your tie is too tight."

"Like?" I said.

"Like, you dumbhead," Renée smiled. "I often wondered what I could do to a nasty slob like you." She took a big sip of her drink, put it back on the bar and walked toward me, the fingers of her hand spread out over the delicious swell of those sleek, wide hips.

"I think you're impotent," she said.

The laugh stayed behind my lips. I put my drink down and looked at her, big and naked and lovely, all nice high titties and a dark curly snatch, her smile almost a sneer, and I said very softly, *"Oh, brother."*

"What?"

"In the Army we said you were ready to be rued, screwed, blued and tattooed."

"You're not doing anything."

"I'm wondering why I should."

"Perhaps you can't."

As carefully as I could I slid off the couch and shrugged my coat off. I picked the .45 out of the shoulder holster and laid the leather on the floor. Then I picked off my tie, unbuttoned my shirt and flicked the belt out of its restraints. My pants were only a hindrance. I let them go around my feet and kicked them aside.

"So you're not impotent," she said after a long, hungry glance.

I sat down on the couch again and picked up my drink. All I had was ice left. "I could have told you that."

"Talking isn't proving."

"Sugar," I told her, "you're forgetting something. There's nothing I have to prove. I get what I want whenever I want it. I can name the time, place and position. Twenty years ago I would have hosed a snake if somebody held it down for me, but now I'm selective. It's

74

still a man's world, baby, but you have to be a man to live in it. Then again, I'm still curious."

Her forehead wrinkled inquisitively. "Curious? About what? There's nothing more to show you unless I turn inside out."

"Don't do that. I just had the rug cleaned." I grinned at her.

Then she laughed, picked up her drink and sat down in my Naugahyde recliner like she was at a presidential reception. "Curious," she said again. Her eyes went up and down me twice, her smile getting broader. "We make a great couple. Naked six feet apart. What can be more curious than that?"

I got up, mixed another drink and went back to the couch again. "Why you came on so strong. This is our second time out, kid. Two hellos and you're ready to go fifteen rounds in the hay. You're class, big business and big money with enough style to snag any guy you want . . ." I held up my hand to cut off her interruption ". . . and suddenly you get the hots for a lousy beat-up old soldier in the shadow police business."

Renée's teeth glistened in her smile and she raised her glass in a mock toast to me. "Crude, but very astute, Mike. But I told you I was going to cultivate you, didn't I?"

I nodded.

"And I told you it would be hard, didn't I?"

I grinned back and adjusted my position. There were times when a guy could be quite uncomfortable.

"So the answer should be obvious," she said. "I enjoy my position, I enjoy my wealth, I take pleasure from my social obligations, but oh, they're so *damned* dull." She nodded toward the window. "There aren't any challenges left out there. I operate on a man's level, but they won't let me get in there and swing. Everybody's so hellishly condescending and polite, patting my head because I did my homework and came up with the right answers. Then when nobody's looking they try to pat my fanny and always seem to miss. Sometimes I wish one of them would get me alone in the stockroom or something."

"Attagirl, tiger," I said.

"Stop laughing. It's serious."

"Why don't you marry William?"

"Because he's already married."

"Oh?"

"To corporate structure," she said. "Commerce is his wife, children and mistress. Women are nothing unless they

75

are an adjunct to the business. We are nutured, tolerated and exploited according to our abilities to perform."

"Come on, honey, you like the guy."

"He's the biggest challenge of all, but the only game you play without any possible chance of winning."

"That sure pigeonholes me, doesn't it?" I asked her.

Renée tried her drink again, then swirled the ice around in the glass, making it clink musically. "Who can win with you, Mike?"

"Nobody, unless I let them," I said.

"Are you going to let me?"

"No."

"You dirty dog. Why not?"

"Right now you're having too much fun sitting here talking about it. The experience is new and exciting. It's like kicks, doll. It's even better than having a guy roped to stakes in the ground and standing over him with a whip. The only thing that bugs you is that I laid down the ground rules."

"What a bastard you are."

"How come everybody says that to me?"

"Because you are. I can even tell what you're thinking." I looked at her and waited.

She said, "You're getting kicks out of it, too, sitting there naked and horny, watching me suffer, knowing damn well there's going to be a next time and when that happens it's going to be something incredible."

"You called me, remember?"

"And I'll call you again." She let her teeth show in another brilliant smile. "I don't care if you *are* a bastard. I wish you didn't know so much about women, though. Tell me one thing, Mike . . ."

"What?"

"You could have stopped it all by having a casual drink with me and turning the conversation into more normal avenues. Why didn't you?"

I finished my drink, studied the empty glass a moment then put it on the floor. "It's been a rough few days, sugar. I lost a friend, got shot at, clobbered, interrogated by . . . oh hell. You were a welcome relief, a lift to the old ego. You have to get up to bat before you know if you can hit or not."

"Now you're going to make me get dressed and send me home," Renée said.

I felt a laugh rumble out of my chest. "Roger, doll. So hate me. You'll always wonder what it would have been like."

76

Her glass went down to the floor too and her laugh had a throaty tinkle to it. "I'll find out. Cultivating you may take longer than I thought. You may turn out to be the biggest challenge of all."

"Not tonight."

"I know. But since you've been such a bastard, will you do something for me?"

"Maybe."

She pushed herself out of the chair slowly, all naked, smooth skin radiating warmth and desire, little pulse beats throbbing erotically in the lush valleys. She reached out, took my hand and encouraged me to my feet until flesh met flesh, insinuating themselves together in a way that only flesh can.

"Kiss me," Renée said. After the briefest pause. "*Hard.*"

I climbed out of bed and stood in front of the window watching the thin patter of rain dribble down the dust-caked glass. The morning crowds were at their desks inside their offices and the shoppers hadn't started out yet. Two blocks away a fire siren howled and a hook and ladder flashed through the intersection, an emergency truck right behind it. *Damn games,* I thought. *I lost a night; I started out for Woody Ballinger and almost wound up doing bedroom gymnastics.* I wiped my face with my hand, feeling the stubble of a beard under my fingers, then grinned at my reflection in the window pane. Hell, I needed the break. Even near-sex could be good therapy. "Buddy," I said out loud, "maybe you still got it, maybe you haven't, but either way they think you have and want some of it."

Okay, so a guy needs an ego boost occasionally.

I switched on the television, dialed in to a news station and went to the bathroom to shave and clean up. I was putting a new blade in the razor when I heard the announcer talk about a shooting during an attempted robbery on West Forty-sixth Street, one that was broken up by a civic-minded passerby.

Thanks, Pat, I said mentally.

While I shaved there was news about the troop movements going into critical areas of the state, sections where power stations and reservoirs were located, their training missions all highly secretive. Results of the operations would be analyzed and announced within two weeks.

Two weeks. That's how much time they knew they had. Success meant announcement. Failure meant destruction.

77

There would be no need for an announcement then.
Somehow I still couldn't get excited about it. I wondered
what the city would look like if the project failed. New
York without smog because the factories and incinerators
had no one to operate them. No noise except the wind
and the rain until trees grew back through the pavement,
then there would be leaves to rustle. Abandoned vehicles
would rot and blow away as dust, finally blending with the
soil again. Even bones would eventually decompose until
the remants of the race were gone completely, their grave
markers concrete and steel tombstones hundreds of feet
high, the caretakers of the cemetery only the microscopic
organisms that wiped them out. Hell, it didn't sound so
bad at all if you could manage to stick around somehow
and enjoy it.

A commercial interrupted the broadcast, then the announcer came back with news of a sudden major-power
meeting of the United Nations. A possible summit meeting
at the White House was hinted at. The dove factions were
screaming because our unexpected military maneuvers
might trigger the same thing in hostile quarters. The hawks
were applauding our gestures at preparedness. Everything
was going just right. Eddie Dandy's bomb was demolished
in the light of the blinding publicity that seared the unsus-
pecting eyes of the public.

And all I wanted to do was find me a pickpocket. Plus
a couple of guys who had tried to knock me off.

I finished my shower, got dressed, made a phone call,
then went down to the cabstand on the corner. Eddie
Dandy met me for coffee in a basement counter joint on
Fifty-third, glad to get away from the usual haunts where
he was bugged about his supposed TV goof. He was sitting
there staring at himself in the polished stainless steel side
of the bread box, his face drawn, hair mussed, in a suit
that looked like it had been slept in. Somehow, he seemed
older and thinner and when I sat down he just nodded
and waved to the counterman for another coffee.

"You look like hell," I said.

"So should you." His eyes made a ferret-like movement
at mine, then went back to staring again.

I spilled some milk and sugar into my coffee and stirred
it. "I got other things to think about."

"You're not married and got kids, that's why," he said.

"That bad?"

"Worse. Nothing's turned up. You know how they're
faking it?" He didn't let me answer. "They've planted
decoy containers in all shapes and sizes that are supposed

78

to be explosive charges. Everybody's out on a search, Army, Navy, C.D. units, even the Scouts. They're hoping somebody will turn up something that isn't a decoy and they'll have a starting place. Or a stopping place."

I grabbed a doughnut and broke it in two, dunking the big end in my coffee. "That bad?"

"Oh, cool, Mike, cool. How the hell do you do it?"

"I don't. I just don't worry about it. They got thousands of people doing the legwork on that one. Me, I have my own problems."

"Like getting shot at in Lippy's apartment."

"You get around, friend."

"There was a news leak out of Kansas City and Pat had me in again. I heard him talking about it to the guy with the squeaky voice from the D.A.'s office. All I did was put two and two togeher. What happened?"

"Nothing." I gave him the details of the episode and watched him shrug it off. Nothing was as big as what he was sitting on right then.

"Maybe you got the right attitude after all," Eddie finally said. He sipped his coffee and turned around. I knew his curiosity would get the better of him. "When you going to ask me something you don't know?"

I stuffed the rest of the doughnut in my mouth, wiped the jelly off my fingers and grinned at him. "Woody Ballinger," I said.

"Come on, Mike." His voice sounded disgusted with me.

"Two months ago you did that crime special on TV," I reminded him. "Part of the exposé touched his operation."

"So what? I made him a typical example of hoods the law doesn't seem to tap out, always with enough loot to hire good lawyers to find the loopholes. He hides everything behind legitimate businesses and goes on bilking the public. You saw the show."

"I'm interested in what you didn't say, friend. You researched the subject. You got some pretty weird contacts too. You were fighting a time element in the presentation and the network didn't want to fight any libel suits, even from Woody."

"Mike ... what's to know? He's in the rackets. The cops know damn well he's number two in the policy racket uptown but can't prove it. It used to be bootlegging and whores, then narcotics until he rubbed Lou Chello wrong and the mob gave him that one-ended split. He has what he has and can keep it as long as his nose stays clean

79

with the lasagne lads. They'll protect their own, but only so far."

"A year ago there was a rumble about buddy Woody innovating a new policy wrinkle in the Wall Street crowd. Instead of nickels and dimes it was a grand and up. Winning numbers came from random selections on the big board. There was a possibility of it being manipulated."

"Balls. Those guys wouldn't fall for it," Eddie reminded me.

"They're speculators, kid," I said. "Legit gamblers. Why not?"

Eddie waited while the counterman poured him another coffee and left to serve somebody else. "I checked that out too. Nobody knew anything. I got lots of laughs, that's all."

"Wilbur Craft supposedly made a million out of one payoff," I said.

"Nobody saw it if he did. Or maybe he paid it to his lawyers to get him off that stock fraud hook. I spoke to him up in Sing Sing and he said it was all talk."

"Maybe he didn't want to get hit with an income tax rap on top of everything else. He only drew three years on the fraud rap."

"Keep trying, Mike."

"Craft still has his estate in Westchester."

"Sure, and the place in Florida and the summer place in Hawaii. It was all free and clear before they rapped him."

"Upkeep, pal. It takes a lot of dough," I said.

"I know. I got a five-room apartment on the East Side."

"Suppose Woody did run a big operation independently?"

"Then he'd be sticking his neck way out there just asking it to get chopped off. The dons would have their pizza punks out there with their shooters in his ears for even trying it. No dice, Mike."

"Guys get big," I said. "They don't want somebody else's hand in their affairs. They think they're big enough to stand them off. They have their own shooters ready to protect the territory."

"Unknown powers can do it. Not slobs who like to parade it in public."

"Egos like to be recognized," I said.

"That's how they get dead."

"Just suppose," I asked him.

Eddie blew on his coffee and tasted it. He had forgotten the sugar, made a face and stirred some in. "He'd have to do it in his head. No books, no evidence. All cash, personal contacts, and hard money payoffs."

"Woody's a thinker, but no damn computer."

"Then a minimum of notations, easy to hide, simple to destroy."

"But it could be done?"

"Certainly, but . . ." Eddie put his cup down and turned around to look at me, his eyes squinted half shut. "Either you're trying to make me feel good by getting my mind off things or you got something. Which?"

"You'll never feel good, kid. I was just confirming something I thought of."

"Damn, you're a bastard," Eddie said with a quick grin.

"*Why* does everybody call me that?" I asked.

CHAPTER 7

Velda had left a recorded message at ten fifteen stating that she had located Little Joe, the no-legged beggar who pushed himself along on a skate-wheeled platform. Little Joe had seen Lippy and a tall, skinny guy together on several occasions. They were obviously friends, but Little Joe didn't buy the other guy at all. He figured him for a hustler, but didn't ask any questions. His own business was enough for him. He could probably recognize the guy again if he saw him, but the skimpy description was the best Little Joe could do. Velda had left him my numbers to call if he saw him again and if it turned up right Little Joe earned himself a quick hundred. Meanwhile, Velda was going to stay in the area and see what else she could pick up.

Tall and skinny. Probably a million guys like that in the city, but at least it was a start. Eliminate the squares, look for a hustler in a ten-block area during a critical time period when the theater crowds were going in and out and you could narrow it down to a handful. The trouble was, that handful would be the cagy ones. They wouldn't be that easy to spot. They had their moves plotted and a charted course of action if somebody made them. They could disappear into a hundred holes and nobody was going to smell them out for you. I put the phone back, turned my raincoat collar up and went outside and waited for a cab.

Pat's office wasn't the madhouse I thought it would be. All officers available for duty were out in the field and only a lone bored-looking reporter was on a telephone turning in a routine report. A dozen empty cardboard coffee cups stuffed with drowned cigarette butts littered the desk, holding down sheafs of paper.

I said, "Hi, buddy," and he turned around, his face seamed with fatigue lines, his eyes red-veined from lack of sleep. "You look beat."

"Yeah."

I pulled a chair up, sat down and stretched my legs. "Since when does an operation this size involve homicide?"

"Ever since that guy died in the subway."

"Anything new?"

"Not a damn thing."

"Then why don't you try sleeping in a bed for a change?"

"We're not all private citizens," Pat growled.

"How's the general reaction so far?"

"We're managing."

"Somebody's going to wonder about the Russians looking for a summit meeting and the bit going on in the U.N."

"There's enough tension in the world to make it look plausible. You have four shooting fracases going on right now and three of those involved have nuclear capabilities if they decide to use them. There's reason enough for international concern. Washington can handle it if certain parties who know just a little too damn much can keep quiet."

"Don't look at me, buddy. It's your problem."

Pat gave me a lopsided grin. "Oh no. Some of it's yours. Unless you're immune to certain deadly diseases."

"They isolate it yet?"

"No."

"Locate the agents that were planted here?"

"No."

"You talk too much," I said.

Pat leaned back and rubbed his eyes. "There's nothing to talk about. For the first time the Reds are as bugged about it as we are. They know we have a retaliation policy and damn well know its potential. Nobody can afford to risk a C.B. war. They haven't been able to run down a single piece of written evidence on this business at all. If there ever was any, it's been deliberately destroyed by that previous regime. That bunch tried to keep a dead hand in office and they did a pretty good job. We have to work on rumor and speculation."

"Did the technicians at Fort Detrick come up with anything?"

His eyes gave me an unrelenting stare.

"Come on, Pat. There's nothing really new about our chemical-biological warfare program being centered there."

"What could they come up with?" he asked me softly.

"Like nuclear physics, problems and solutions seem to

83

be arrived at simultaneously. When that agent was planted here that bacteriological program would have been developed to a certain point. Now it's twenty-some years later, so they should be able to guess at what he had as a destructive force."

"Nice," Pat said. "You're thinking. They can make a few educated guesses, all right, but even back then, what was available was incredibly destructive. Luckily, they worked on antibiotics, vaccines and the like at the same time so they could probably avoid total contamination with a crash immunization program."

I looked at him and grinned. "Except that there isn't enough time to go into mass production of the stuff."

Pat didn't answer me.

"That means only a preselected group would be given immunization and who will that group consist of ... the technicians who have it at hand, a power squad who can take it away from them, or selection by the democratic method of polls and votes?"

"You know what it means," Pat said.

"Sure. Instant panic, revolution, everything gets smashed in the process and nobody gets a thing."

"What would you do, Mike?"

I grinned at him again. "Oh, round up a few hundred assorted styles of females, a couple of obstetricians, a few male friends to share the pleasure and to split the drinks, squirt up with antibiotics and move to a nice warm island someplace and start the world going again."

"I never should have asked," Pat said with a tired laugh. "At least now I'll be able to get some sleep knowing the problem has been solved." He yawned elaborately, then stifled it. "Unless you got another one."

"Just one. Did ballistics get anything on those shots in Lippy's apartment?"

Pat moved a coffee cup aside and tugged out a stained typewritten sheet of paper. "They dug a .38 slug out of the floor. The ejected cartridge was a few feet away. The ring bands on the lead were well defined so it was either a new piece or an old gun with a fresh barrel. My guess would be a Colt automatic."

"You check the sales from local outlets?"

"Peterson did. Everything turned up clean since the new law in the state went into effect, but prior to that there were thousands of sales made outside the state that would be almost impossible to run down. Anybody intending to use a gun illegally is going to be pretty cagy about it, especially buying one through a legitimate source. I wouldn't pin any hopes on tracking that job down unless you locate the gun itself. Or have you?"

"Not yet."

"I wish I had the time or inclination to nail your pants to a chair," Pat said. "Right now I couldn't care less. Incidentally," he added, "I might as well give you a little fatherly advice. Although several people in rather high places who seem to know you pretty well have vouched for your so-called integrity, the skeptics from the bureaus in D.C. decided a little surveillance wouldn't hurt. They didn't like the contact between you and Eddie Dandy this morning."

"I didn't have any tail on me."

"Eddie did. He works in a more sensitive area than you do. It wouldn't surprise me a bit if he went into custody until this thing was over."

"They wouldn't be that stupid."

"Like hell they wouldn't. He tell you about that business in Kansas City?"

"He mentioned it."

"Plain luck we stopped it this time."

"It'll get a lot stickier if anybody *really* wants to get inquisitive," I said. "How about some lunch?"

"Thanks, but I'm too bushed. I'm grabbing some sleep. Tonight I got a detail covering the reception at that new delegation building they just opened. The Soviets and their satellite buddies are throwing a bash and everybody's got visions of fire bombs and bullets dancing through their heads."

"Crazy," I said. "Can I use your phone?"

"Go ahead."

I dialed my office number, waited for the automatic signal, held the tone gimmick up to the mouthpiece and triggered it. Four faint musical bleeps came out, there was a pause and a voice with a laugh hidden in it said, "Please, Mr. Tape Recorder, inform your master that his cultivator is available for an afternoon drink. He has the office phone number."

I felt myself grinning and hung up.

"Has to be a broad," Pat said. "It has to."

"It was," I told him.

"Just how many broads you figure you collect any given month, pal?"

"Let's put it this way," I said. "I throw away more than most guys get to see."

85

Pat wrinkled his face and waved for me to get the hell away from him. Some perennial bachelors are different from others.

The bar at Finero's Steak House was packed three deep with a noisy crowd fighting the martini-Manhattan war, the combatants armed with stemmed glasses and resonant junior-executive voices. A scattering of women held down the barstools, deliberately spaced out to give the stags room to operate, knowing they were the objects of attention and the possible prizes. The one on the end was nearly obscured by the cluster of trim young men jockeying for position, but for some reason the back of her head and the way her hair tumbled around her shoulders was strangely familiar to me. She swung around to say something and laugh at the one behind her who was holding out a lighter to fire up her cigarette when her eyes reached out between the covey of shoulders and touched mine.

And Heidi Anders smiled and I smiled back.

The two young men turned and they didn't smile because they were Woody Ballinger's two boys, Carl and Sammy, and for one brief instant there was something in their faces that didn't belong in that atmosphere of joviality and the little move they instinctively made that shielded them behind the others in back of them was involuntary enough to stretch a tight-lipped grin across my face that told them I could know.

Could.

From away back out of the years I got that feeling across my shoulders and up my spine that said things were starting to smell right and if you kept pushing the walls would go down and you could charge in and take them all apart until there was nothing left but the dirt they were made of.

So I made a little wave with my forefinger and Heidi Anders said something to her entourage, put her glass down on the bar and came to me through the path they opened for her and when she reached me said, "Thank you, Mike."

"For what?"

"Yelling at me. I looked in the mirror. It's worse than the camera. It tells you the truth without benefit of soft lighting, makeup men and development techniques."

"Sugar," I asked her, "when did you last pop one?"

"You were there."

"And it was cold turkey all the way? Kid, you sure don't look like you're in withdrawal."

A flash of annoyance tugged at her eyes and that beautiful mouth tightened slightly. "I had help, big man. I went for it right after you left. Dr. Vance Allen. You've heard of him?"

I nodded and studied her. Vance Allen wasn't new to me. He was a longtimer in the field of narcotic rehabilitation. Some of his measures were extreme and some not yet accepted into general practice, but his results had been extremely significant.

"Hurt any?"

"At first. You're looking at an experiment with a new medication. In a way I'm lucky. I wasn't hooked as badly as you thought."

"Who put you on it?"

"That's one of those things I'd rather not talk about. In time it will be taken care of. Meanwhile, I'm working at being unhooked."

I shook my head and looked past her. "Not yet. Right now you're nibbling at another line."

Heidi tilted her face and squinted at me, not understanding.

"That pair you're with are a couple of hoods."

"Oh . . . don't be silly." She gave me a disgusted grimace. "They work for Mr. Ballinger and Mr. Ballinger . . ."

" . . . is a legitimate businessman," I finished for her. "One day try old issues of the newspapers . . . about July, four years ago, or check into your nearest friendly precinct station. The desk sergeant will fill you in on his background."

"I don't believe . . ."

"You got any reason *not* to believe me?"

"No." But her voice was hesitant.

"Somebody tried to kill me last night." I looked past her to the bar again and she almost turned to follow my gaze.

"But . . ."

"When you go back there," I said. "tell your friends that I'll be looking them up. Right after I see their boss. We have a little business to discuss too."

Some of the color drained out of her face and she gave an annoyed toss of her head, her lower lip pinched between her teeth. "Damn! You men . . ."

"Just tell them, Heidi."

"I don't know why . . ."

"Tell them. And have the message passed on to Larry Beers too."

I winked at her and left her standing there a moment watching me before she walked back, that wild hip-swaying walk reflecting her annoyance. Carl and Sammy weren't going to be too happy with the news. They'd been too used to doing the chasing and calling the shots when and where they wanted them.

The maître d' and headwaiter had seen Woody Ballinger earlier, but he had left about an hour ago. His office secretary had called a little while back looking for him, so he wouldn't be there. I just told them that they could tell Woody Mike Hammer was looking for him on a "business matter" and if he didn't find me I'd find him. Let Woody sweat a little too.

Between three and four in the afternoon the New York cabbies change shifts. It's bad enough on a nice day trying to fight the women shoppers and the early commuters for one, but in the rain, forget it. You could stand in the street and get splashed by their wheels or try walking, but either way you'd get soaked. For once the weathermen had been right and they were predicting three more days of the same. Intermittent heavy rain, occasional clearing, windy and cool. It was a hell of a time to be on the streets.

A girl walked by the store entranceway I was nestled in, head lowered into the slanted rain, her plastic coat plastered to her body, outlining her scissoring thighs as she doggedly made her way to the corner to make a green light. At least she reminded me of something. I went inside the store, bought a pack of cigarettes, walked back to the phone booth, put a dime in the slot and dialed a number.

The secretary told me to hold, checked me out, then put Renée Talmage on the line. She chuckled once and said, "Hello, teaser."

"But fun, kid."

"Too frustrating, but yes ... fun. At least different. Where are you?"

"A couple blocks away and soaking wet."

"There's a nice little bar downstairs in the building where you can dry out while we have a drink."

"Fine," I told her. "Five minutes."

It was closer to fifteen and she was part of the way through a cocktail, totally engrossed with the bartender in a discussion about the latest slump in the stock market, when I got there. I tossed my soggy trench coat and hat on the back of a chair and climbed on the barstool next to her. "Must be great to be intelligent. Bring me a beer," I told the bartender.

She stopped in the middle of Dow-Jones averages and tilted her head at me. "And I thought you had class. A beer. How plebeian."

"So I'm a slob." I took the top off the beer and put the glass down with a satisfied burp. "Good stuff, that. You have to raise your hand to get out of class?"

"Recess time." She laughed and sipped her cocktail. "Actually, the day is done. William is socializing with the wheels of the world and I'm left to my own devices for the time being."

"You got nice devices, kid," I said. The dress she had on wasn't exactly office apparel. The vee-neckline plunged down beside the naked swell of her breasts to disappear behind a four-inch-wide leather belt. "Don't you have anything on under that?" I asked her.

"We women are exercising our newfound freedom. Haven't you heard about the brassiere-burning demonstrations?"

"Yeah. I heard. Only I didn't figure on being this close to the ashes. It's distracting."

"Well?"

"Don't guys find it hard to keep their eyes off you?"

Renée looked at me with an amused smile, her mouth formed into a tiny bow. "Very hard."

"Cut it out."

Her smile got deeper. "Me? You're the one making all the dirty remarks."

I almost spilled my beer before I managed to get it down.

"Now what have *you* been doing to get so wet . . . tailing a suspect?"

"Not quite. There are better ways of nailing them. I've been walking and remembering a dead friend who shouldn't have died and thinking out why he died until things begin to make a little sense. One day, one second, it's all going to be nice and clear right in front of me and all those targets will be ready to be knocked off."

The funny little smile on her face warped into a worried frown and some deep concern showed in her eyes. "Is it . . . that personal, Mike?"

"All the way."

"But you're serious . . . about killing."

"So was somebody else," I told her.

89

Renée looked into her glass, started to raise it, then put it down and looked at me again. "Strange."

"What is?"

"My impressions. I read about people in your line of work, I see the interpretations on TV and in movies ... it's rather hard to believe there really *are* people like that. But with you it's different. The police ..."

"Cops are dedicated professionals, honey. They're in a tough, rough, underpaid racket with their lives on the line every minute of the day. They get slammed by the public, sappy court decisions and crusading politicians, but somehow they get the job done."

"Mike ... I thought I knew people. I'm personally responsible for the actions and decisions of several thousands and answerable only to William Dorn. I can't afford to make mistakes in selecting them for sensitive positions, but I would have made a mistake with you."

"Why?"

"Because ... well, there are different sides of you that nobody can truly see."

"You've just lost touch with the lower class, kid. You work on too high a level. Get out there on the street where the buying public is and you'll see a lot of other faces too. Some of them probably work for you too. Not everybody is in an executive position. Macy's and Sears Roebuck still do a whopping big business by catering to their tastes."

"Take me with you, Mike," she said.

"What?"

"You could be right. I'd like to see these people."

"Renée, you'd get your clothes dirty, your nails broken, and your ass patted. It's different."

"I'll survive it."

She was so serious I had to laugh at her. I finished the fresh beer the bartender set in front of me and thought, what the hell, a change of pace could be good for her. It was one of those evenings where nobody was going anyplace anyway, so why not? We could cruise through the entrails of the city and maybe pick up pieces here and there that were lying around loose.

Down at the end the bartender had switched on the TV to a news station and the announcer finished with the weather and turned the program over to the team who handled the major events. Somebody in Congress was raising a stink about the expenses involved in calling up National Guard and Army Reserve units for a practice maneuver that apparently had no meaning. Film clips taken by some enterprising photographer who had slipped past the security barrier showed uniformed figures slogging through mud and water, flashlights probing the darkness. Another shot had a group locating and dismantling some apparatus of destruction around a power station. He even included the information that they were deliberately planted decoys with a minimum explosive capacity to sharpen the soldiers' abilities. It seemed that most of the activity was centered around the watershed areas in key areas across the nation with chemical analysis teams right in the thick of things. The commentator even speculated briefly on sophisticated chemical-biological warfare techniques and this exercise was possibly for training in detection and neutralizing an enemy's attack from that direction.

He never knew how nearly right he was.

Tom-Tom Schneider's killers had escaped a trap laid by the Detroit police. Somebody had passed the word where they could be found and there was a shoot-out in the Dutchess Hotel. Two cops were wounded, a porter killed, and it was believed that one of the suspects was shot during the exchange. An hour later a known police informer was found murdered with three .38's in his chest along a highway leading from the city. It was going to make a good pictorial spread in tomorrow's papers.

The mayor was screaming for more crime control and was setting up a panel to study the situation. Good luck, mayor.

"Great world out there," I said.

"I'd still like to see it with you."

"Okay. Finish your drink."

I hoped I wouldn't run into Velda. Women don't exactly appreciate other women's plunging necklines.

Caesar Mario Tulley was a professional panhandler who bused over from Patterson, New Jersey, every day, picked up a hundred bucks in nickles and dimes from the tourist suckers, then went back to his flashy suite in a midtown hotel. He had pageboy hair, a faceful of stringy whiskers and a motley outfit of clothes held together with beads and chains that no decent hippie would be caught high in. But it was his gimmick. That and the lost look in the young-old face and tired eyes. The women felt sorry for him and the men flipped their quarters in his hand to pay for the snide remarks that went with the coin. Hell, he probably was making out better than any of them.

He saw me and Renée squeezed together under her

umbrella, half stepped out of the shoe store doorway, then recognized me and those deliberately tired eyes pepped right up. A loose-lip grin split the whiskers and he said, "Oh, hi, Mike. Almost put the bite on you."

"Fat chance," I told him. "How you doing, Caesar?"

"Lousy tonight. Tried working Radio City and got rousted by the fuzz. Then some drunk belts me in the chops figuring I was his own kid and tried to drag me back to Des Moines, Iowa. I was halfway to the Forty-second Street subway before I shook him loose. What kind of kooks they got around here these days?"

"Look in the mirror, kid."

"Man, I'm straight! A working stiff! You think I'd go this route if it didn't pay off! Twice a week I take acting classes and already I got a future lined up. You see me on TV the other night?"

"Great show." Last Tuesday they did a special on the hippies in town and managed to round up a few of the real pros like Caesar. Twenty-seven runaway kids in Greenwich Village were recognized and picked up by their parents, four narcotics pushers were spotted by sharp-eyed detectives and hauled in on possession charges, and the public had a good idea of what the city was coming to.

"Pig's ass it was a good show," Caesar said sullenly. "Practically everybody spots me. I even got a call from the Internal Revenue Service. Making it ain't so easy now."

"So act."

"What do ya think I'm doing? It ain't Shakespeare, but it sure takes talent."

"And nerve." Renée smiled.

"Lady, come on. It's all part of the game." He rattled his beads and stepped back into his doorway shelter again. "What you doing out, Mike?"

"Trying to find somebody. Tall, skinny, in his forties and boosting wallets in the theater district. Got anything?"

He cocked his head and peered at me, eyes squinting. "Hey, some hustler was asking the same thing. Big chick, long dark hair, real knockout. Don't know why she was hustling, but I tried to make out and she brushed me off. Me! How about that? I wanted to give her a twenty . . ."

"You would have had your head handed to you," I said, grinning again. Caesar boy had run into Velda.

"Fuzz?" he asked, incredulously.

I nodded, not explaining all of it.

"Man, they sure make them real these days. She coulda

busted me for panhandling. Awful pretty for fuzz though, even under that face crap."

"The guy I mentioned, Caesar?"

"Hell, I don't butt in to somebody else's . . ."

"You buck the theater crowds, Caesar. He would have been in the same area."

He shrugged, giving a small negative shake to his long hair, but his eyes didn't want to look at me. I stepped out from under the umbrella and got up close to him. "Compared to withholding information, panhandling is a chintzy rap."

"Mike . . . you ain't the fuzz. You . . ."

"My license makes me responsible to turn certain facts over to them, buddy."

"Hey, I thought we was pals."

"After office hours."

Caesar Tulley made a resigned gesture and ran his fingers through his hair. "There was some talk. Wooster Sal saw this guy hit a couple of joes and tried to cut himself a chunk. He got a busted lip for it."

"You see him?"

"I saw him pop Wooster Sal. Like a sneak punch. Wooster shoulda kept to his own racket."

"Anything special about him . . . facial characteristics . . . you know?"

Another shrug. "Just a guy. I didn't get a real good look. Anyway, I didn't want one. I'm opposed to violence."

"What about this Wooster Sal?"

"Hell, after that he dug out for the West Coast. Gone like two weeks now."

"Keep looking, okay? I'm in the phone book."

I flipped him a wave and started to walk away when he called me back. "Hey, Mike, there was one thing."

I turned and waited.

"He wore a red vest. Pretty dumb in his business."

One more little piece to add to the pile. In time it would mount up to a face and a body. One red vest, and it probably wasn't dumb. It was a good luck charm, vanity or any other of a dozen reasons a petty crook could consider imperative.

I hooked my arm through Renée's and pushed the edge of her umbrella out of my face. "You have odd friends, Mike. Those newsstand dealers, the pair at the hamburger stand . . . who else do you know?"

"You'd be surprised," I said. "Still feel like prowling?"

Renée glanced at her watch and tightened her hold on

my arm. "It's almost ten, my big friend. I told you I had to meet William at that reception in a half hour."

It was the same one Pat had mentioned to me, the opening of the new Soviet delegation buildings. "Since when are you people messed up in politics?"

"Since Teddy Finlay from the State Department invited us. One of the new delegates was a foreign supplier for our Anco Electronics before we bought him out. Finlay thought it would be beneficial to have a less formal introduction to him."

"And where do you come in?"

"I pick up William's memos he made at the meeting today, give him his tickets for his Chicago trip tomorrow, murmur a few pleasantries and leave." Impulsively, she added, "Why don't you come along?"

"We aren't exactly in evening clothes, baby."

"But we won't be going to the reception proper. I'm to meet him in office A-3 in the west annex, not where the crowd will be. Please, Mike?" She nudged me expectantly, her leg touching mine in a long-legged stride. The wind gusted and blew the rain under the umbrella into my face. Hell, it would be good to get out of it for a few minutes.

"Why not?" I said.

The two uniformed cops covering the annex entrance scanned Renée's admittance card and checked our ID's. The older one, sweating under his rubber raincoat said, "Hold a second," then walked across the street to a squad car, talked through the window and stepped back when the door opened. I let out a grunt of amusement when Pat got out, hunched against the rain, his hands in his pockets.

When he saw me his face finally registered something besides tired boredom. "Now what are *you* doing here?" he asked me.

"Personal invitation, old buddy."

"His name isn't on the card," the cop told him. "What do you think, Captain? The dame's okay."

Pat flipped the rain from the brim of his hat and stepped away, nodding for me to follow him. He swung around, his voice a low growl. "This stinks. No matter what you tell me, it plain stinks. What are you building?"

"Not a thing, Pat. Miss Talmage has a business appointment with her employer there and invited me along. Can anything be simpler?"

"With you, nothing's simple," Pat said. "Look, if you pull anything . . ."

"Unwind, will you buddy? Can't I talk to you any more?"

For a long few seconds he studied my face, then let a smile crack the corners of his mouth. "Sorry, Mike. I guess I got too much bugging me. There's more than one meeting going on in there."

"So the Soviets really are cooperating on that C.B. deal?"

"You called it. And they're scared stiff. All the top brass from Fort Detrick arrived at seven with a limousine of Russkies straight off a chartered nonstop plane from Moscow right behind them."

"Military types?"

"Hardly. Some were too old for that."

"Specialists in chemical-biological warefare," I suggested.

"Could be."

"Any newspapers covering it?"

"Only the social end. They missed the first batch. That's why you spook me. Nothing better interrupt that meeting."

"Quit worrying about me. Anything turn up yet?"

"One lonely probability. A couple on a honeymoon camping trip spotted a guy wandering around the Ashokan watershed area. He seemed to be sick . . . kind of stumbling, fell a couple of times. They were going to go over to him but he wandered up to the road and must have thumbed a ride. The rough description they gave was similar to the guy we found in the subway."

"The Guard in the area?"

"Like a blanket. Boats, divers, foot by foot search. They cut off the water flow from that district and that they *can't* keep a secret, so they'd better come up with some imaginative excuse before morning."

"Oh, they will," I said casually.

Pat jammed his hands back into his pockets and grimaced in my direction. "They better do better than that. Right now you can realize what it's like to be in death row with no reprieve in sight."

"Yeah, great," I said. "By the way, you ever get tipped to a pickpocket who works in a red vest?"

"Go screw your pickpocket in a red vest," Pat said sourly. He waved an okay sign to the two cops and headed back toward his car.

The ramrod-stiff butler with the bristly gray hair scrutinized the admission card, verified Renée with an inaudible phone call and apparently described me after giving my name. The reply was favorable, because he took our

95

wet clothes, hung them in a closet in the small foyer and led us to the office door in the rear. Unlike my coat, his hadn't been tailored to conceal a heavy gun and it bulged over his left hip. For him, butlering was a secondary sideline. He had been plucked right off an army parade ground.

William Dorn introduced me to the five of them as a friend of his, his eyes twinkling with amusement. They all gave me a solemn handshake, the one-jerk European variety with accented "How-do-you-do's" except Teddy Finlay. He waited until Dorn and Renée were exchanging papers and the others talking animatedly over drinks, then pulled me aside to the wall bar and poured a couple of highballs.

He handed me one, let me taste it, then: "How long have you been a 'friend' of William, Mike?" He laid it heavy on "friend" so I'd know he made me.

"Not long," I said.

"Isn't being here an imposition?"

"Why should it bother you? The State Depatment doesn't work on my level."

"Mr. Robert Crane is my superior. It seems that you were trying to work on his. Nobody is pleased having you know what we do."

"Tough titty, feller. Crane didn't like it because I wouldn't take his crap. I won't take yours either, so knock it off."

"You still didn't answer my question." There was a hard edge in his voice.

"I have a contract to bump the Russian Ambassador. That sound like reason enough?"

"One phone call and you can be where Eddie Dandy is, Mr. Hammer."

I took another pull of my drink, not letting him see how tight my fingers were around the glass. "Oh? Where's that?"

"On vacation . . . in protective custody. He was getting a little unruly too."

When I finished the drink I put the glass back on the bar and turned around to face him, the words coming quietly from between my teeth. "Try it, stupid. I'll blast a couple of .45's into the ceiling and bring every damn cop and reporter around in this joint. Then just for fun I'll run off nice and fat at the mouth and really start that panic you're working your ass off to avoid. That loud and clear?"

Finlay didn't answer me. He just stood there with white

lines showing around his mouth and his forehead curled in an angry frown. Two of the Czech representatives had been looking curiously in our direction, but when I turned, faking a smile, they stopped watching and went back to their conversation. Dorn and Renée had finished their business and were laughing at some remark Josef Kudak had made and waved me over to join them. Kudak was the new member of the Soviet satellite team, but it was evident that the three of them were old friends despite political differences.

"Good joke?" I asked.

William Dorn chuckled and held a match to a long, thin cigar. "My friend Josef thinks I'm a filthy rich, decadent capitalist and wants to know how he can get that way too."

"Tell him?"

"Certainly not. I bought him out for three million dollars and I'd wager he hasn't spent a penny of it yet."

"You don't know my wife *or* our tax structure, friend William," the Czech said. He was a small, pudgy man with a wide Slavic face and bright blue eyes. "Between them they have reduced me to poverty."

"There are no poor politicians," I put in.

Renée looked startled, but Dorn laughed again and Kudak's face widened in a broad smile. "Ah," he said, "at last a candid man. You are right, Mr. Hammer. It is all a very profitable business, no? Should it be otherwise? Money belongs to those who can get it."

"Or take it," I said.

"Certainly, otherwise it would rot. The peasants put their gold into little jars and bury it. They die of old age without revealing where they have hidden it, so afraid are they of having it stolen. With it they buy nothing, do nothing. It is for the businessmen, the politicians to see that money is kept circulating."

It was hard to tell if he was joking or serious, so I just grinned back and lit up a smoke. "I wish some of it would circulate my way."

Kudak's eyebrows went up a little in surprise. "You are not a politician?"

"Nor a good businessman," I added.

"But you must have a profitable specialty ..." He looked from me to Dorn and back again.

"Sometimes I kill people," I said.

Dorn let out a long laugh at the expression on Kudak's face and the way Renée grabbed me to make a hurried exit after a quick handshake with everybody I'd met. When she got me outside in the rain she popped her umbrella open with typical feminine pique and said, "Men. They're all crazy!" She stretched her arm up so I could get in beside her. "What a thing to say to a man in high office. Doesn't anything ever embarrass you?"

"Wait till he finds out it's true," I said.

"I'll never take you with me again."

"Never?"

"Well, at least not where there's people. Now, where are we off to?"

I looked at my watch. It was twenty after eleven and raining. Inside the main building the reception was going full force and the sound of a string quartet was almost drowned out by the steady hum of voices. On the street at least fifty uniformed cops stood uncomfortably in assigned positions waiting for their shift to end. Pat's car was gone, but the pair of harness bulls still stood at the fenced entrance. It was the kind of night when New York slept for a change. At least those who knew nothing of the man in the subway.

And maybe the guy in the red vest.

I turned my coat collar up and threw my cigarette into a puddle where it fizzled out. "Suppose I check my office, then we go out for supper."

"No more prowling?"

"I've had enough for one day."

I signed us in at the night desk and steered Renée to the open elevator on the end of the bank, got in and pushed the button for my floor. She had that impish grin back, remembering the look the night man had given us downstairs, and said, "The direct approach is very fascinating, Mike. Do you have a couch and champagne all ready?"

"No champagne. Might be a six-pack of Pabst beer in the cooler though."

"How about a bathroom? I have to piddle."

"And so ends a romantic conversation," I said as the door slid open noiselessly.

"Well, I really have to," she insisted.

"So go," I told her.

She was taking little mincing steps walking down the corridor to my office, and to make sure nothing would stay between her and the john, I got ahead, stuck my key in the lock and pushed the door open.

Not really pushed. It was jerked open with me leaning on the knob and I tumbled inside knowing that the world would be coming down on my head if all the reflexes hadn't been triggered in time. But there are some things

98

you never seem to lose. They drilled them into you in the training camps, and made you use them on the firing line and what they didn't teach you, you learned the hard way all at once or you never lived to know about anything at all. I was in a half roll, tucking my head down, one hand cushioning my fall and the other automatically scrabbling for the .45 when heavy metal whipped down the back of my head into my shoulders with a sickening smash. Then you know there's still time because the pain is hot and wet without deadening numbness and the secondary impulses take over immediately and whip you away from the force of the second strike.

I was on my back, the flat of my hand braced for leverage, bringing my foot up and around into flesh and pelvic bone in a high, arching kick that gouged testicles from their baggy sockets with a yell choked off as it was sucked down a throat in wild, fiery agony. I could see the shadowy figure, still poised for another smash at my head, the bulk of a gun in his hand, then it jerked toward me convulsively and the flat of my .45 automatic met frontal bone with all the power I could put behind it. Time was measured in tenths of a second that seemed to take minutes, but it was enough to buy me time. Two blasts of flame went off in my face, pounding into the back of the one on top of me and something tore along the skin of my side, then Renée was screaming in the doorway until another shot rocketed off and cut it off abruptly. I saw the other one run, saw her fall, but couldn't get out from under the tangle of limp arms and legs that smothered my movements in time. Crazy words spilled from my mouth, then I got the body off me, pushed to my feet with the .45 still cocked and staggered into the corridor.

Down the hall the blinking lights of the elevator showed it was almost halfway to the ground floor. None of the others were operating and I could never beat it down the stairway. I shoved the gun back in the speed rig under my coat and knelt down beside Renée. She was unconscious, her eyes half open, a heavy red welt along her temple, oozing blood where the bullet had torn away hair and skin. She was lucky. In her fright she had raised her hands and the heavy ornamental knob of the umbrella handle had deflected the slug aimed for her face and turned sudden death into a minor superficial scratch. I let her lie there for a minute, went back into my office and switched on the light.

The body on the floor was still leaking blood that soaked into the carpet and all I could think of was that the next time I'd get a rug to match the stains and save cleaning costs. I put my toe under the ribs and turned it over. The two exit wounds had punched gaping holes in the chest and the slash from my rod had nearly destroyed his face, but there was enough left to recognize.

Larry Beers wouldn't be renting his gun out to the highest bidders any more. One slug that had gone right through him and grazed me was still imbedded in the carpet, a misshapen oval of metal standing on edge. There were no alarms, no sirens, no voices; the office building was deserted and we were too high up for gunshot sounds to reach the street.

I stood up and looked around at the absolute destruction of all my new furniture, the mess of cotton batting from torn cushions, papers from the emptied files and remnants of furniture that had been systematically destroyed. But they had started to work from one side to the other and stopped three quarters of the way across. I knew what had happened. They had located the automatic taping system built into the wall behind the street map of New York City. Somebody had played it. Then somebody had destroyed it. The ashes were still warm in the metal wastebasket in the corner of the room.

Like a sucker punch in the belly the picture was clear. There was a call on that tape, probably from Velda. It meant something damn important, enough to kill for. Now one was dead, but the other was still loose and if Velda had identified herself they'd know who to look for and probably where. If she had gotten hold of something she'd want to meet me and would have set a time and a place.

Larry Beers, Ballinger's boy. Out of curiosity I looked at the bottom of his shoes, saw the half-moon-shaped pieces of metal imbedded in the heels that old lady Gostovitch had called clickers and felt good because one was down who deserved it, and the one paying the price would be the guy who ran off and the one who was paying for the hit. It was Woody I had to find before he found Velda. There was one little edge I still had, though. They couldn't be sure I wasn't dead, and if I wasn't I'd be looking for Woody too, and he had to reach me fast because he knew he'd be on my kill list just as sure as hell.

Behind me a small, frightened voice said, "Mike . . ."

Renée was standing in the doorway, hands against the frame, her face white and drawn. She saw the body on the floor but was still too dazed to realize what had happened. She tried a painful smile and lifted her eyes. "I . . . don't think I like your friends," she said.

CHAPTER 8

There was no way of determining the actual cause of the wound, so the doctor accepted her explanation without question. The tip of an umbrella whipped in a sudden cross-directional gust had caught her, we said. He applied an antibiotic, a small compress she hid behind her hair and had me take her home. She still had a headache, so she took the sedative the doctor had given her, a little wistful at me having to leave, but knowing how urgent it was that I must. She had been caught up in something she had never experienced and couldn't understand, but realized that it wasn't time to ask questions. I told her I'd call tomorrow and went back into the rain again. My shirt was still sticking to my side with dried blood, stinging, but not painful. That could wait. The doctor never saw that one because he would have known it for what it was and a report would go in.

Back in the office a body still sprawled on the floor in its own mess, a note to Velda on its chest to check into the hotel we used when necessary and hold until I contacted her. The door was locked, the "OUT" sign in place, now Woody Ballinger could sweat out what had happened.

The night clerk in the office building had heard the elevator come down, but was at the coffee machine when the occupant left the lobby and all he saw was the back of a man going out the door. Four others had signed the night book going in earlier and he had assumed he was one of those. When I checked the book myself the four were still there on the second floor, an accountancy firm whose work went on at all hours. Woody's boys had it easy. A master key for the door, time to go through my place and time to phone in whatever information they found on the tape. Then they just waited. They couldn't take the chance of me getting that message and knew that if I did I'd want to erase it on the chance that Woody

101

would make a grab for me after I made it plain enough to his boys that I was ready to tap him out.

Okay, Woody, you bought yourself a farm. Six feet down, six long and three wide. The crop would be grass. You'd be the fertilizer.

I stood under the marquee of the Rialto East on Broadway, watching the after-midnight people cruising the Times Square area. The rain had discouraged all but a few stragglers, driving them home or into the all-night eating places. A pair of hippies in shawls and bare feet waded through the sidewalk puddles and into the little river that flowed along the curb, oblivious to the downpour. One lone hooker carrying a sodden hatbox almost started to give me her sales pitch, then obviously thought better of it and veered away. She didn't have to go far. A pair of loud, heavyset conventioneer types had her under their arms less than a half block away. What they needed around here was the old World War II G.I. pro stations. Nowadays the streetwalkers carried more clap than a thundercloud. Syph was always a possibility and galloping dandruff a certainty.

Earlier, a dozen phone calls to the right people had gotten me the same piece of information. Woody Ballinger had been missing from the scene ever since this morning. Carl, Sammy and Larry Beers were gone too. I had lucked into snagging the apartment Carl and Sammy shared, but the doorman told me they had left in the morning and hadn't returned. He let me confirm it myself by rapping on their door.

And now I was worried. Nobody had seen Velda since four hours ago. Her apartment phone didn't answer and the place she had taken opposite Lippy's old place was empty. The small bag she had taken with a few extra clothes was in the closet, two sweaters on hangers and a few cosmetics on the ancient dresser beside the bed.

When she worked in the field, Velda was a loner. Except for a few personal contacts, she didn't use informants and stayed clear of places she would be recognized. But Woody knew her and if she were spotted it wouldn't be too hard to grab her if they went at it right.

I knew what she was wearing from what was left over in her luggage and had passed the word around. Denny Hill was pretty sure he had seen her grabbing a coffee and a hot dog in Nedick's, but that had been around seven o'clock. I found Tim Slatterly just closing his newsstand and he said, sure he had seen her early in the evening. She was all excited about something and he had made change for her so she could use the phone in the drugstore on the corner.

"Thought she was a hooker." Tim laughed. "You shoulda seen the getup she had on." He pulled off his cap, whipped the rain off it and slapped it back on again. Then he looked at me seriously. "She ain't really . . ."

"No. She was on a job for me."

He let the smile fade. "Trouble?"

"I don't know. You see which direction she came from?"

Tim nodded toward the opposite side of Seventh Avenue going north. "Over there. I watched her cross the street." He paused a second, rubbing his face, then thumbed his hand over his shoulder. "Ya know, this probably was the closest place to call from. Two blocks up is another drugstore and one block down is an outside booth. If this one was closest she probably came from that block right there."

So she was in a hurry. She wanted to make a phone call. *That could have been the one to me recorded on the tape that was destroyed.* And what she found could have come from that direction.

"You see her come out, Tim?"

"Yeah," he nodded. "She had a piece of paper in her hand. At first she started to flag down a cab, then gave it up and headed back over the West Side again. Look, Mike, if you want I'll call over to Reno's and the guys can . . ."

"It'll be okay, buddy. Thanks."

"Oh . . . and Mike, she ever find that guy? The one with the fancy vest? She asked me about that too."

"When?"

"That was, lemme see . . . right after I came on this morning. Like I told her, I see them things sometimes. One guy been coming here eight years always wears one. He owns a restaurant downtown. Rich guy. There's another one, but he kind of drifts by once in a while at night. I figured him for a pimp."

I edged back under the protection of the overhang, the rain draping a curtain around us. "Tall and skinny, about forty-some?"

Tim bobbed his head quickly. "Yeah, that's him."

"When did you see him last?"

"Hell, about suppertime. He was still drifting along when everybody else was hustling to get outa the wet. I remember because the bum picked a paper outa the trash

103

can somebody tossed away instead of buying one. A wet paper yet." Tim stopped, watching me intently, then added, "So he started to cross the street heading west too. I wasn't really watching."

"Good enough, Tim," I said.

And now the reins were pulling in a little tighter. The possibilities were beginning to show themselves. It was me who had put Woody onto it in the beginning. He had his own sources of information and it wouldn't have taken him long to spot the association between Lippy and me and dig around the same way I did. If I had found anything Lippy's former friend had lifted from Woody, the police would have had it by now and he'd be squatting on an iron bunk in the city jail.

But no charges had been leveled, so whatever he was after was still up for grabs. I let the rain whip at my face and grinned pointlessly. So he double-checked Lippy's pad with his boys and they damned near knocked me off. They had taken off fast, not knowing how long I had stayed around, and maybe if I looked hard enough I could have uncovered the item. It wouldn't be big. Large enough for a wallet and easy enough to hide.

It made sense then. They had to take me out to be sure. They ransacked my office first, then waited for me. They had to. After my bit earlier about "doing business" with Woody, he could have assumed I had the stuff and was ready to sell it to him. That would be "business" in his language. Or Velda could have come up with it and phoned in the information on the tape recorder and they couldn't take a chance of me getting it. They'd try to tap me out first, then Velda.

Damn it all to hell, why didn't she stay in the office where she belonged?

From a quarter mile down the avenue came a whine of sirens and tiny red dots winked in the night. I waited and watched another convoy of Army trucks rumble by, escorted by two prowl cars clearing the way. All of them were way above the speed limit. The last four were ambulance vehicles and a jeep. When they passed by I crossed to the other side of Seventh Avenue and started working my way west across town.

At four A.M. I checked out a single lead and came up with a guy in a red vest, a stew bum conked out on wine, sleeping in a doorway on Eighth Avenue. I said something under my breath and walked down to the bar on the corner that was just about to close up for the night. I tried Velda's apartment first, but there was no answer. I tried the hotel I wanted her to use, but nobody using our cover names had checked in. My office phone rang twice before it went to the recorder with the fresh spool I had inserted. There were no messages. By now Larry Beers' corpse would be cold and stiff, his blood jellied on the floor. Pat was going to give me hell.

He did that, all right, standing there over the body and chewing me out royally, his eyes as tired and bloodshot as my own. Outside the windows the sky had turned to a slate gray, the rain had stopped, but poised and waiting until it could be at its most miserable best when it let loose again.

The body of Larry Beers had been carted off in a rubber bag, the room photographed, the basics taken care of, now two detectives were standing outside the door getting a muffled earful as Pat lit into me.

All I could say was, "Listen, I told you I had a witness."

"Fine. It better be a good one."

"It is."

"You better have a damn good excuse for the time lapse in reporting this mess too."

"Once more for the record, Pat, my witness got hurt in the shuffle. I took her to a doctor who will verify it."

"He had a phone."

"So I was in a state of shock."

"Balls. You know the kind of lawyer Ballinger has to protect his men? You think that other guy's going to admit laying for you? Like hell . . . they'll say you set a trap and touched it off youself deliberately in front of a witness. Nice, eh? You were even supposed to get the other one, but he got away. So maybe your bullets aren't in him. The other guy was firing in self-defense."

"Look at the office."

"You could have done that yourself. You told me you didn't see them in the act of wrecking it. Your witness couldn't help there, either."

"Well, you know better."

"Sure, *I* do, only I'm just a cop. I can investigate and arrest. I don't handle the prosecution. Your ass is in deep trouble this time. Don't think the D.A.'s office is going to buy your story on sight. What you *think* happened won't cut any grass with that bunch. Even the shooting at Lippy's won't help any. That could have been staged too. You try using the witness you got there and all you'll get is a cold laugh and a kiss-off. Even your own lawyer wouldn't touch them."

105

"Okay, what do you want from me?" I asked him.

"Who's your witness, damn it!"

I grinned and shrugged my shoulders. "You know, you forgot to advise me of my rights, Captain. Under that Supreme Court decision, this case could be kicked right off the docket as of now."

Pat let those red eyes bore into me for ten seconds, his teeth clamped tight. Then suddenly the taut muscles in his jaw loosened, he grinned back and shook his head in amazement.

"I don't know why I'm bothering with you, Mike. I'm acting like this is the first homicide I ever stumbled over. After all the nitheaded times you and I ... oh, shit." He swabbed at his eyes with his hands and took a deep breath. "The whole damn country's in line for extermination and I'm letting you bug me." He dropped his hands, his face serious. "Anyway, by tomorrow you wouldn't even make the back page."

I didn't say anything. His face had a peculiar, blank look.

Finally, Pat dropped his voice and said, "They found a canister at the bottom of the Ashokan Reservoir. It was a bacteriological device timed to open six days from now."

I couldn't figure it. I said, "Then why the sweat if you got it nailed down?"

Pat brushed some torn remnants off the arm of the chair and lowered himself down to it. "The guy found dead in the subway was the same one those honeymooners spotted, all right. They searched the area where they saw him and came up with the cannister." His eyes left the window and wandered over to mine. "It must have been the last one he planted. It was marked #20—ASHOKAN. Someplace scattered around are nineteen others like it, all due to release in six days."

"And the papers got this?"

"One of the reservists in the group that handled the stuff was a reporter fresh out of journalism school. He figured he had a scoop and phoned it in. He didn't know about the other nineteen they didn't find."

"There's still time to squelch the story."

"Oh, they're on that, don't worry. Everybody connected with that guy's paper is in protective custody, but they're screaming like hell and they're not going to be held long. There's a chance they might have spouted off to their friends or relatives, and if they did, it's panic time. People aren't going to hold in a secret like that."

"Who's handling it ... locals?"

"Washington. That's how big it is." Pat reached for his hat and stood up. "So whatever you do doesn't really matter, Mike. You're only an interesting diversion that keeps me from thinking about other things. Six days from now we can all pick out a nice place to sit and watch each other kick off."

"Brother, are you full of piss and vinegar tonight."

"I wish you'd worry a little. It would make me feel better."

"Crap," I said sullenly. There was no mistaking Pat's attitude. He was deadly serious. I had never seen him like that before. Maybe it was better to be like the rest of the world, not knowing about things. But what would they be like when they found out?

"Six days. When it happens you can bet there's going to be some kind of retaliation, or expecting it, the other side fires first. A nuclear holocaust could destroy this country and possibly the bacteria too. If I were on the other side I'd consider the same thing." Pat let a laugh grunt through his teeth. "Now even the Soviet bunch is thinking along those lines. I heard they all tried to get out of the country when we found the thing, but the Feds put the squeeze on them. In a way they're hostages for six days and they'd better run down a lead before then or they've had it too."

"Sounds crazy," I said.

"Doesn't it?" Pat waved me to the door. "So let's have a coffee like it all never happened and then we'll check into the ballistics report on those slugs that tore up your buddy Beers."

I lay stretched out on the bed, not quite awakened from the druglike sleep I had been in. The window was a patch of damp gray letting the steamy smells of the city drift into the room through the open half. The clock said ten after two, and I pulled the phone down beside me and dialed the office number. Nothing. Velda's apartment didn't answer either.

Where the hell was she? Until now Velda had always called in at regular intervals, or if necessity warranted it, longer ones, but she always called. Now there were only two answers left. Either she was on a prolonged stakeout or Woody Ballinger had found her. I tried another half-dozen calls to key people I had contacted, but none of them had seen Woody or any of his boys. All his office would say was he had left town, but Chipper Hodges had gone into his apartment through a window on a fire escape and said his bags were in a closet and nothing seemed to be missing.

Pat had slept in his office all night and his voice was still a hoarse growl with no expression in it at all. "Sorry, Mike," he said, "still negative. Nobody's seen Ballinger around at all."

"Damn it, Pat . . ."

"We'd *like* to see him, though. Ballistics came up with another item besides those slugs in Beers coming from that same gun that shot at you in Lippy's apartment. That same gun was used to kill the cop who stepped into the cross fire when he was raiding that policy place uptown. Supposedly one of Woody's places."

"And now you got men on it."

"Uh-huh. As many as we can spare. Don't worry, we'll find Ballinger."

"He might have Velda. There isn't much time."

"I know," he told me softly, "not for any of us," then hung up.

Back to *that* again, I thought. Six days . . . no, five days left. In a way there was almost a comic angle to the situation. The ones who didn't know what was impending couldn't care, and those who knew about it didn't. A real wild world, this. Trouble was coming in from so many sources that another one, no matter how big, was no more than an itch to be scratched. Maybe the world wouldn't give a damn either if it did know. Nobody seems to think that big. *Sufficient unto the day are the evils thereof.* How long since Hiroshima and Nagasaki? You sit on a time bomb so long you get to ignore it. The object of destruction gets to be a familiar thing and one more wouldn't matter anyway. Defusing the problem was somebody else's job and somehow in some way it would be taken care of. That's what we have a government for, isn't it? So why worry, have another beer and watch the ball game. The Mets are ahead.

I picked up a paper at the stand on the corner and riffled through the pages. The *News* had a two-column spread on page four about how the special Army teams in their exercise maneuvers upstate had located a possible contamination source in the Ashokan Reservoir, and although the water supply to New York City and adjacent areas had been temporarily curtailed, there was no actual shortage and the Army experts were expected to clear the matter up shortly.

Further on was another little squib about a certain Long Island newspaper suspending operations temporarily due to a breakdown in their presses. Washington was putting the squeeze on, but good. I wondered how Eddie Dandy was making out, wherever he was. By now he must have a mad on as big as his head. Somebody was going to catch hell when they released him, that was for sure.

Little Joe was working his trade on Broadway, pushing himself along on a homemade skateboard. For a beggar he was ahead in his field, peddling cheap ball-point pens instead of pencils, gabbing with all the familiar figures who kept him in business with the daily nickels and dimes.

I drew his attention by fluttering a buck down over his shoulder into his box and he spun around with a surprised grin when he saw me. "Hey, Mike. Thought I just got me a big spender. You want a pen?"

"Might as well get something for my dollar."

He held up his box. "Take your pick."

I pulled out two black ones and dropped them in my pocket. "Velda told me she saw you," I said.

"Yeah," Joe said, craning his neck up to look at me. "She was looking for that dip I saw with old Lippy."

A curious tingle ran across my shoulders. "She didn't say what he was. You didn't know, either."

"That was *then*. Me, I ain't got much to do except look, and besides, you two always did get me curious. So I look and ask a few people and pretty soon I get a few answers. Since Lindy's closed I moved my beat up here a couple of blocks and you'd be surprised how much can go on just a pair of traffic lights away. Like another world."

"Don't yak so much, Joe."

"Mike . . . when do I get the chance to? Like you're a captive audience." Then he saw the impatience in my face and nodded. "He came in from Miami about two months ago where he was working Hialeah. That was his thing, working the tracks where the cash money was and the crowds and the excitement. Only the security boys made him and he got the boot."

"Who fed you that?"

"Banjie Peters. He hustled tout sheets. He even knew the guy from a few other tracks that kicked him out. So the only place he don't get the boot is Aqueduct and he comes up here for the season. He works it one day and blammo . . . security spots him and gives him the heave. He was lucky because he didn't even have time to make his first touch. They find him with anything on him and it's curtains out there."

"They have a name for him?"

"Sure, a dozen, and no two alike." He gave me a funny

109

little grin and fished around in his legless lap for something. "I kind of figured you'd be around so I had Banjie con his buddies in security outa a picture they had. They mugged him at Santa Anita and sent copies around."

He held out a two-by-two black and white photo of a lean, sallow-looking face with a mouth that was too small and eyes that seemed to sneer at the world. His hair had receded on the sides and acne scars marred the jawline. The picture cut him off at chest level, but under his coat he had on an off-shade vest with metal buttons that could have been red. His description on the back put him at age forty-six, five feet eleven tall and one hundred fifty-two pounds. Eight aliases were given, no two remotely alike, and no permanent address.

Now I knew what he looked like.

Little Joe said, "He couldn't score at the track, that's why he started hustling around here. You remember Poxie?" While I nodded Joe went on. "When he ain't pimping he keeps his hand in working other people's pockets. This boy sees him working Shubert Alley and beats the crap outa him. Like he laid out a claim and was protecting it. Over there's where he and Lippy used to meet up. You know, Mike, I don't think Lippy knew what the guy was doing."

"He didn't," I said.

"Maybe he found out, huh? Then this guy bumped him."

"Not quite like that, pal. You know where he is now?"

"Nope, but I seen him last night. He come outa one of them Greek language movies on Eighth Avenue and hopped a cab going uptown. I woulda taken the cab number so you could check out his trip sheet, only I was on the wrong side of the street."

"Good try, kid."

"If you want, I'll try harder."

I looked at him, wondering what he meant.

Little Joe grinned again and said, "I saw Velda too. She was right behind him and grabbed the cab after his."

The knot in my stomach held fast, not knowing whether to twist tighter or loosen. "What time, Joe?"

"Last show was coming out. Just a little after two-thirty."

And the knot loosened. She was still on her own then and Ballinger hadn't caught up with her. She had located our pickpocket and was running him down.

Little Joe was still looking at me. "I saved the best until last, Mike," he said. "The name he really goes by is

110

Beaver. Like a nickname. He was in Len Parrott's saloon when Len heard two guys ask about him. This guy drops his drink fast and gets out. They were asking about a red vest too and the guy had one on." A frown drew his eyebrows together. "They was Woody Ballinger's boys, Mike."

I said, "Damn" softly.

"The bartender didn't tell them nothing, though."

I let a five-spot fall into Little Joe's box. "I appreciate it, buddy. You get anything else, call Pat Chambers. Remember him?"

"Captain Pat? Sure, how could I ever forget him? He shot the guy who blew my legs off with that shotgun fifteen years ago."

If you can't find them, then let them find you. The word was out now in all the right places. It would travel fast and far and someplace a decision would have to be made. I was on a hunt for Sammy and Carl to throw a bullet through their guts and do the explaining afterward. They'd start to sweat because there was plenty of precedent to go by. I had put too many punks they knew under a gun for them to think I wouldn't do it and the only way to stop it would be to get me first. They were the new cool breed, smart, polished and deadly, so full of confidence that they had a tendency to forget that there were others who could play the game even better. Who was it that said, *"Don't mess around with the old pros"*?

I finished straightening up the wreckage in the office, pulled a beer out of the cooler and sat down to enjoy it. From the street I could hear the taxis hooting and thought about Velda. She was a pro too and it would take a pretty sharp article to top her. She knew the streets and she knew the people. She wasn't about to expose herself and blow the whole job no matter how far into it she had gotten. If the chips went down, she'd have that little rod in her hand, make herself a lousy target and take somebody down too. At least in New York you heard about shootings.

I switched on the transistor radio she had given me and dialed the news station. For ten minutes there was a political analysis of the new attitude the Russians had taken, seemingly agreeable to acting in harmony with U.S. policy along certain peace efforts, then the announcer got into sports. Halfway through there was a special bulletin rapped out in staccato voice telling the world that the hired killers of Tom-Tom Schneider had been located in a

111

cheap hotel in Buffalo, New York, and police officers and F.B.I. troops had surrounded the building and were engaged in a gunfight, but refraining from a capture attempt because the pair had taken two maids as hostages.

Okay, Pat, there's your news blast for tomorrow. Plenty of pictures and plenty of stories. It would cover all news media in every edition and the little find at the Ashokan Reservoir would stay a one-column squib that nobody would notice and you had one more day without a panic.

There was a four-car wreck on the West Side highway. A mental patient leaped from the roof of an East Side hospital, landed on a filled laundry cart and was unhurt. No other shootings, though, and the regular musical program resumed.

All I could do was wait awhile.

At six thirty in the morning I woke up when my feet fell off the desk. Daylight had crept into the office, lighting the eerie stillness of a building not yet awake. There was a distant whine of the elevator, probably the servicemen coming in, a sound you never heard at any other hour. I stood up, stretched to get the stiffness out of my shoulders and cursed when a little knife of pain shot across my side where the slug had scorched me. Two blocks away a nice guy I knew who used to be a doctor before they lifted his license for practicing abortions would take care of that for me. Maybe a tailor could fix my jacket. Right now the spare I kept in the office would do me.

At eight fifteen I picked up the duplicate photo cards Gabin's Film Service had made up for me, mug shots of the guy they called Beaver with his résumé printed on the back. A half hour later I was having coffee with Pat and gave him all but three of them.

He called me two dirty names and stuck them in his pocket. "And you said you wanted nothing to do with it," he reminded me.

"Sorry about that," I said.

"Yeah. Professional curiosity?"

"Personal interest."

"You're still out of line. Regulations state you're supposed to represent a client." He dunked a doughnut in his coffee and took a bite of half of it.

"Be happy, friend. I'm giving you no trouble, I'm paying for the snack and staying out of your way. You should be glad citizens take an active interest in affairs like this. Besides, you haven't got the time."

"So why the photos?"

"You still have routine jobs going. Pass them along to

the plainclothes boys. Maybe you got bigger things on your mind, but this is still an open murder."

"For you it's not open."

"I'm just throwing back the foul balls."

"Mike," he said, "you're full of shit. Sometimes I wish I had never known you."

"You worry too much, friend."

"Maybe you should. The days are going by fast."

I took a close look at his face. The lines were deeper now, his eyes a lined red, and when he spoke it was almost without moving his lips. Somehow he couldn't focus on me, seeming to look past me when he spoke. "Our Soviet friends have come up with another piece of information. When we wouldn't let them out of the country they really began digging. That strain of bacteria the former regime packaged and sent here was more virulent than even they suspected. If it's loose there's no hope of containing it, none at all. The lads at Fort Detrick confirmed it and if we don't get a break pretty damn quick it's all over, Mike, all over."

"That doesn't sound like police information."

"Crane broke down when he got the news. I was there when he went hysterical and blew it."

"How many others know this?" I asked him.

"You're the eleventh." He finished the doughnut and sipped at his coffee. "Kind of funny. We sit here like nothing's happening at all. We want a pickpocket in a red vest, I watch the teletype to see how they're doing in Buffalo with those contract hoods, everybody else is plugging through the daily grind and in a few days we'll all be part of the air pollution until nature figures a way out of it in a couple million years."

"Man, you're a happy guy today."

Pat put the cup down and finally got his eyes fixed on mine. "Mike," he said, "I'm beginning to figure you out."

"Oh?"

"Yeah. You're crazy. Something's missing in your head. Right now I could lay odds that all you're thinking about is a dame."

"You'd lose," I said. I picked up the tab and stood up. "I'm thinking about two of them."

Pat shook his head disgustedly again. "Naked?"

"Naturally," I said.

CHAPTER 9

Something had happened to the Broadway grapevine. Nobody had seen Velda and although a half-dozen of the regular crowd were able to spot the red-vested Beaver by his photograph, nobody had seen him either. Woody Ballinger, Carl and Sammy were in the nothing pocket too and I was beginning to get those funny little looks like it was *"Watch out, Mike, you're tangling with the trouble crowd now"* time. Not that it was a new experience, but they were beginning to watch and wait, hoping to be there when the action started.

Some people liked car races. You could see the big kill happen there too. Others took it where they could find it, and now they were beginning to get a blood smell and watched the field leaders to see who was going to crowd who in the turn and wind up in pieces along the walls of Manhattan. By noon the sunny day had turned overcast again, the smog reaching down with choking little fingers, and I had reached Lexington Avenue where I had another cup of coffee in a side-street deli just to get out of it.

The counterman used to work for Woody and he couldn't give me a lead at all. It was nearly my last straw until I remembered how close I was to that crazy pad in the new building just a few blocks away, and finished the coffee and picked up a pack of butts at the cashier's desk while I paid my bill. There was somebody else who knew the people I was looking for.

The doorman flipped a fingertip to his cap and said, "Afternoon, sir."

"Your partner still courting?"

"He'll never learn. Last night he got engaged. I do double shifts and don't get any sleep, but I'm sure making the bucks. Just wait until he starts buying furniture."

"Miss Anders in?"

"Sure. Different girl, that. Something happened to her. Real bright-eyed now. I think maybe she dumped that

114

clown she was going with. Playboy, no good at all. Too much money. Last night she got in at ten, and alone. You want me to call up, officer?"

I grinned at him, wishing Pat could have been here. He would have turned inside out. To Pat I was always the other side of the fence, with my face always the prime type to get picked up in a general dragnet.

"Don't bother," I said. I returned his casual wave and walked to the elevator.

Heidi Anders saw me through the peephole and snapped off the double locks on the door. It opened a scant three inches on the chain and that pert face with the tousled ash-blonde hair and full-lipped mouth was peering at me with a disguised smile and I said, "Trick or treat?"

The door closed and I heard the chain come off. When it opened again her head was tilted in a funny smile, the upslanted eyes laughing at me. "Trick," she said. Then added, "But if you come in, it'll be a treat."

"I'll come in."

She let the door open all the way and I walked inside. I was treated. Heidi Anders was standing there bare-ass naked, prettier than any centerfold picture in a girlie magazine and no matter how lovely those uniquely rounded breasts were, or how all that ash-blonde hair contrasted, all I could see was that crazy navel with the eyelashes painted around it like an oversexed Cyclops.

"I just got up," she said.

"Don't you ever take your makeup off?"

"It's part of my personality," she told me. "Most men have an immediate reaction." She closed and locked the door behind me. "I wish you had."

"I want to wink at it."

"At least that's different." She smiled and walked down the hall, not bothering to take my hat this time. That wild gait was still there, but naked it had a totally new sway. I let her get all the way into the living room before I moved. Then I went in slowly, watching all the corners just to be sure, glad to have been in enough games not to get wiped out at the first charge of the opposition.

She didn't know it, but my hand was hooked over my belt, the palm comfortable against the butt of the .45. Too many times naked women and death walked side by side.

Heidi had thrown back the draperies and stood there in the cold gray light that brought out the tan marks on the flesh, then turned around slowly to face me. "Do I look different, Mike?"

The navel still watched me. Crazy eye. Blind, but crazy and watching. The lashes were extra long.

"Different," I said.

"You did it. You yelled at me. Mike ... you were pretty rough."

"A broad like you shouldn't get hooked on H. There's too much going for you." I picked a cigarette out of my deck and lit it up. "Sorry about yelling at you."

"It wasn't that." She picked up something filmy from the chair and drew it through her hands. "I saw your face when I turned you off. I was lying there all ready and waiting and I turned you off. That never happened to me before. I wanted to get laid and I was right there waiting for you and I turned you off. You yelled. I felt like ... you know what I felt like?"

I nodded. "No retractions, kid."

"Good. We did well, the doctor and I."

"How about Woody Ballinger's goons?"

For a second I thought I had played it wrong, then she kinked her lips in a tiny smile and her eyes lit up again. "I asked around," she said. "You were right, you know."

I reached up and slipped my hat off casually, and held it in front of me. "Will you get dressed?"

I got that grin again. "I asked around about more than Woody Ballinger." Once more I got that provocative, tilt-headed glance. "I didn't think you were so sensitive." Then she sway-walked over to me and held out her hand. "Can I take your hat?"

"Don't be smart-ass," I said. "Just make me a drink."

"They were right." She stepped back and looked at me with feigned wide-eyed amazement. "They were really right."

But she made the drinks, a long cooler for me and a short one for herself, and sat down opposite me in all that colorful nudity and crossed her legs like she was at a tea party in a Pucci dress and let me have the full impact of that little eye in her navel that never blinked and just looked at me with an unrelenting stare.

"Uncomfortable?" she asked flippantly.

But age has its benefits and experience its knowledge. I tossed my hat on the couch and grinned at her. "Nope."

Her smile turned into a mock frown. "Damn, I hate you older men. You have too much control. How do you do it?"

"Science, kitten."

"Impossible."

"See for yourself."

116

"I do but I don't believe it. How can I turn you on again?"

"By quitting the damn hippie talk and answering some questions."

Heidi raised her glass and tasted it, her eyes on mine. "One favor deserves another."

"Where's Carl and Sammy? And Woody?"

Her glass stopped just short of her mouth. "What?"

"You heard me."

"But . . ."

"I told you to pass the word along."

"Mike . . . I told them what you said."

"No reaction? No nothing? You aren't the type of broad they pick up at a bar and not one they leave alone. Those damn slobs can buy tail or crook a finger and it'll come running out of their stables for them. You're a class broad and for you they'll give an excuse. They were both on the make the other night and the way they were pushing they wouldn't just bust out of a date. Where are they, Heidi?"

Her fingers were stiff around the glass and she had tucked her lower lip between her teeth, looking at me intently. "Mike . . ."

"Think," I said.

"Sammy . . . he . . . well, he wanted to see me again and we, well, we sort of made a date, but he called and said it would have to wait."

"Why, honey? Girls don't let a guy off the hook that easily."

"Woody wanted him to . . . do something. He couldn't cancel it."

"Has he called again?"

She nodded, glanced at her drink, then put it down. "Today. An hour ago, I guess."

"Where was he?"

"He didn't say. All he told me was that he'd see me tonight. His job would be done then."

"Where'd he call from?"

"I don't know."

"Damn it, think!"

"Mike . . ."

"Look," I told her. "Remember back. Was he alone? Quiet?"

"No," she said abruptly. "It was noisy, wherever he was. I could hear the tooting."

"Tooting?"

"Well, it was like two toots, then while we were talking, three toots."

"What the hell is a *toot?*" I asked her.

"A toot! You never heard a toot? A horn toot. No, it was a whistle toot. Oh, balls, I don't know what was tooting. It just tooted. Two, then three."

"Heidi . . ."

"I'm not drunk and I'm not high, damn it, Mike . . ."

"Sorry." I let a little grin seep out. How the hell can you get sore at a naked dame four feet away who was so excited she even forgot and uncrossed her legs like she had a dress on. "He say when he was going to see you?"

"Just tonight." She saw the look on my face and frowned too. "If it helps . . . he said he'd call me today sometime to let me know when."

"There are a lot of hours in the day, kid."

"Well, I got mad and said I'd be gone all afternoon and if he wanted to call me it had better be before noon."

I looked at my watch. Noon was an hour away. And in an hour anything could happen. "Let's wait," I said.

Heidi grinned and picked up her drink again. The eye in her navel seemed to half close in its own kind of smile and never stopped watching me. She got up with studied ease, little muscles rippling down her thighs, her breasts taut and pointed and came across the few feet that separated us. Very gently she sat down on my lap.

"Hurt?"

"No," I said.

"Ummmm." Heidi finished the drink and tossed the empty glass on the sofa, then turned around, her hand behind my neck. "I really don't want to see Sammy anyway, Mike."

"Do it for me."

"I owe you more than that."

She squirmed and the glass almost fell out of my hand. She was all sleek and sweet smells and the heat from her body emanated in all directions like some wild magnetic force. Her hand found mine and pressed it against her stomach and all the concerted thought I had had for what was happening outside started to drift away like smoke in an updraft and her mouth kept coming closer and closer, the lips rich and red and wet.

But the phone rang, that damn, screaming, monstrous necessity with the insistent voice that demanded to be answered.

I had to push her to her feet, put her hand on the receiver and wait another second until the shock of the change registered sadly in her eyes.

"Get it," I said.

She picked up the phone, my ear close to hers at the receiver. "Hello?"

The voice was partly hoarse, a muffled voice trying to be heard over some background noise. "Heidi?" Something rumbled and I heard three short faraway sounds and knew it was what she had called *toots*.

"Hello . . . Sammy?" she asked.

Then there was another voice that said, "You crazy!" and the connection was chopped off abruptly.

Heidi let the phone drop back into its cradle, her face puzzled. "It was him."

"Somebody didn't want him making a call," I said.

"I heard those toots again."

"I know. They're blasting warnings around construction sites. Three of them was the all-clear signal."

"Mike . . ."

I reached for my hat, feeling the skin tight around my jaws. "He won't be calling back, Heidi. Not right now."

Someplace things were coming to a head and here I was fiddling around with a naked doll, letting her wipe things right out of my mind. I picked up the phone, dialed my office number and triggered my recording gimmick. One call was from a West Coast agency wanting me to handle some Eastern details for them, the other was from a local lawyer who needed a deposition from me, and the third was from William Dorn who wanted me to call him as soon as possible. I let the tape roll, but there was nothing from Velda or anybody else. I broke the connection, waited a second, then dialed Dorn's office. His secretary told me that he had been trying to reach me, but had gone to a meeting in his apartment thirty minutes ago and I should try him there. She gave me the number and his address and hung up. When I dialed his place the phone was busy, so I gave it another minute and tried again. It was still busy. I said to hell with it, hung up and slapped my hat on.

Heidi had made herself another drink, but none for me. She knew it was over now. I said, "Tough, kitten. It might have been fun."

She took my hand and walked the length of the corridor, then turned and stood on her toes, all naked and beautiful, and reached for my mouth with hers. I let my hands play over her gently, my fingers aching with remorse because there wasn't time to do all the things I wanted to do with her.

Gently she took her mouth away and smiled. "Another day, Mike?"

"Another day, Heidi. You're worth it now."

"I think it will be something special then."

My fingers squeezed her shoulder easily. "Dump those bums of Woody's."

"For you, Mike, anything." She stepped back two paces, an impish grin teasing her mouth, and did something with her stomach muscles.

That nutty eye that was her navel actually winked at me.

The doorman in the towering building on Park Avenue was an old pro heavyweight decked out in a blue uniform trimmed with gold braid that was too tight across his shoulders and his face was enough to scare off anybody who thought they could cross those sacred portals without going through the elaborate screening process that was part of the high rent program.

He half-stepped to intercept me when I came through the glass doors and I said, "Hi, Spud. Do I say hello or salute?"

Spud Henry squinted at me once, then stepped back with a grin that made his face uglier but friendlier and held out a massive paw to grip mine in a crushing handshake. "Mike, you old S.O.B.! How the hell are you?"

"Back to normal when you let go my hand." I laughed at him. "What're you doing here? I thought you had saved your money."

"Hell, man, I sure did, but try retiring around that old lady of mine. She drives me bats. All the time wants me to do somethin' that don't need doin'. *Take the garbage out.* What garbage out? *Who cares, take it out. Paint the bathroom.* I just painted the bathroom. *The color stinks. Get those kids outa the back yard.* Whatta ya mean, get 'em out, they're our kids. Man, don't never get married. It was easier fightin' in the ring."

"How many kids you got, Spud?"

"Twelve."

"How old's the youngest?"

"Two months. Why?"

"Some fighting you do."

Spud gave me a sheepish grin and shrugged. "Well hell, Mike, ya gotta take a rest between rounds, don't ya?" He paused and cocked his head. "What you doin' up this way? I thought you was a side-street type."

"I have to see William Dorn. He in?"

"Sure. Got here a little while ago. He got a crowd up there. Some kind of party?"

120

"Beats me. What's his apartment?"

"Twenty-two, the east terrace. Real fancy place. Since when you goin' with the swells?"

"Come on, Spud, I got a little class."

"That's *big* class up there, Mikey boy. Man, what loot, but nice people. Big tippers, always polite, even to me. Just nice people. When the last kid was born he gimme a hundred bucks. One bill with a fat one-zero-zero on it and it was like the days back in the Garden when they used to pay off in brand-new century notes. You want me to announce you?"

"Never mind. He called me. I didn't call him."

"Take that back elevator. It's express. Good to see you, Mike."

"Same here. Tell the missus hello."

I got off at the twenty-second floor into an elaborate gold-scrolled and marble-ornamented vestibule that reeked of wealth only a few ever got to know, turned east to a pair of massive mahogany doors inlaid with intricate carvings and set off with thick polished brass fixtures. I located the tiny bell button set into the frame, pushed it and waited. No sound penetrated through the doors or walls, nothing came up from the street and I didn't hear anything ring. I was about to touch it again when bolts clicked and the door opened and William Dorn stood there, a drink in one hand and a sheaf of papers in the other.

His surprise was brief, then he pulled the door open and said, "Mike . . . good to see you. Come in. I didn't know you were on the way up."

I didn't want to get Spud in a jam so I said, "I slipped by the doorman while he was busy. Sneaky habit I can't get out of."

Dorn laughed and closed the door. From the other room a subdued murmur of voices blended into a monotonous hum. I could see the backs and shoulders of a dozen men in quiet conversation and when one looked around I spotted Teddy Finlay with Josef Kudak beside him and a few feet away the six-foot-six beanpole from the Ukraine who made all those anti-U.S. speeches in the United Nations last month. This time they all seemed to be pounding at one nail with no disagreement for a change.

"Didn't mean to break in on your party," I said.

"Business meeting," Dorn told me. "Glad you could come. Let's go into the library where we can talk. Care for a drink?."

"No thanks."

He folded the papers in his hand and stuffed them in his pocket. "This way."

The library was another example of class and money. It was there in rare first editions and original oils, genuine Sheraton furniture giving obeisance to a great Louis XIV desk at one end of the room that nestled there like a throne.

"You ever read all those books?" I asked Dorn.

"Most of them." He waved me to a chair. Before I got comfortable he asked, "What happened to Renée?"

"She got creased by a bullet."

Dorn nearly dropped his drink. His mouth pulled tight and I saw his shoulders stiffen. "She didn't tell me ..."

"Don't worry, she's okay."

"What happened?"

"Nothing I'm going to talk about right now. Why?"

"She ... well, she's important to me, damn it. Right now we have a big expansion move on and ..." He looked at me, shook his head and glanced down at his hands that were clasped together too tightly. Finally he looked up. "It might be better if you said what you were thinking, Mike. I'm a callous person so wrapped up in business and finance that nothing else matters. Nothing is expected to interfere with those vital affairs."

"Don't sweat it, William. She'll be okay."

"Is she ..."

"Just a crease. She was real lucky. I'm surprised she didn't tell you about it."

"Renée can keep a confidence, even from me. I knew she was with you, but it was unlike her to ..."

"It was justified. Hell, doesn't she ever get sick?"

"Never."

"A dame got to get her period once in a while. That's usually a good excuse."

"Not with Renée. She treats ... commerce, let's say, almost as I do. You're the first one she ever took an active interest in."

"You don't know what you're missing," I said.

For a second a flash of annoyance creased his eyes, then disappeared into a wry smile. "You may be right. I've heard that before." He picked up a pencil and tapped it against the polished wood of the desk. "Mike ... do me a favor."

I nodded.

"Check on her. She won't answer the phone and I'd rather not bother her after what you just told me."

"Be glad to."

"And Mike ..."

"If it can be avoided, don't expose her to ... well, anything more in your line. I'd appreciate that."

"I didn't expose anybody. It just happened. She wanted to see how we lived on the other side of the tracks. I could have told her it could be just as rough where she came from too because I've been on the other side of the bridge myself. Nobody ever seems to learn anything, do they?"

The seconds ticked by while he looked at me, finally nodding agreement. "And you, Mike. Do you ever learn?"

"Always something new," I said. I got up and took a last look at all the money that surrounded me. "I'll check in on Renée for you. She'll be fine, so quit worrying."

Dorn held out his hand and I took it. "Sorry you couldn't get me at the office. I didn't mean for you to go out of your way. I guess it really wasn't that important after all."

"No trouble," I said.

He walked me to the door and behind me the hum of voices had grown louder. One was edgy and hoarse, but I recognized it as Crane's from the State Department. The one he was talking to said, "Nyet, nyet!" then subsided while Crane finished talking. I said "So long" to Dorn at the door, took the elevator back down again and looked for Spud. He was gone, and a tall kid with a sad face had replaced him. He had his hair tucked under the back of his visored cap and didn't look happy about it. They probably even made him shave off his beard. He couldn't have run off a Bowery panhandler.

Rain. Someday they'd cover New York like the Astrodome and you wouldn't have to worry about it. The computers had predicted partly cloudy and had sat back in their oiled compartments with all the whirring and clacking, giving off with mechanical laughter at the idiots who had believed their programming. The smart one knew the city. Never predict New York. Never try to outthink it. The damn octopus could even control the weather and when it wanted everybody to be miserable, everybody was miserable.

I looked up at the tops of the buildings and watched the gray blanket of wet sifting down to slick the streets and fog the windows, wondering why the hell I didn't get out like Hy Gardner did. A cab pulled up and disgorged a fat little man who threw a bill at the driver and trotted across the sidewalk to the protection of the building entrance and

123

before the elderly couple frantically waving at the cabbie from the corner could make the run, I hopped in and closed the door. The driver saw my face in the rearview mirror and didn't try for the Sweetest Cabbie of the Year award. I gave him Renée's address and sat back while he pulled out into the traffic and U-turned at the corner to head north.

The ends. Why the hell don't they meet? It wasn't all that complicated, just a simple rundown of a lousy pickpocket who lost his haul to an honest guy who tried to keep him straight and killed to get it back. A lousy pickpocket who had hit the wrong pockets and now there were others looking for him too, but why? What did Woody Ballinger have to lose? Heidi Anders had a compact with her life wrapped up in white powder in a false bottom. She would have done anything for a single pop of the junk and damn near did until I creamed her out. Now it was Woody trying to beat me to Beaver.

The driver's radio blared out another of those special bulletins the networks loved to issue. In Buffalo, New York the police had shot and killed Tom-Tom Schneider's killers. The hostages were unharmed. Tomorrow the papers and TV would carry the full account and Pat Chambers could count on another day free of panic. But where the hell was Velda? Where was that lousy dip Beaver in the red vest and where were Woody Ballinger and his boys? The rain splattered against the windows and the radio went back to Dow-Jones averages and the cab pulled into the curb. I peeled off a five from my roll and handed it through the window to the driver.

The little patch on her head around the shaved area of her scalp was nearly unnoticeable, her hair covering it with the usual feminine vanity. I grinned at her, lying there under the covers and she smiled back, her eyes twinkling, "I know," she said, "under the covers, the nightgown . . . I'm stark naked."

"Lovely," I said.

"X-ray eyes?"

"Absolutely. I walk down Fifth Avenue and all those broads in their fancy clothes think they're hiding something? Hell, I look right through them and all I see is skin and hair and toenails that need cutting. Everybody's naked, sugar."

"Am I naked?"

"My X-ray eyes are out of order."

Renée looked at me and smiled, then pushed the

124

covers down to her midriff, then all the way to her feet with a quick flip of her hand. Without taking her eyes off mine, she tugged at the nightgown, then slipped it over her head and tossed it to the floor.

"*Now* you're naked," I said.

"You don't sound excited."

"I'm an old dog, kid. I had this happen before lunch." I lit up a butt and took a deep drag, then let the smoke blow across the bed.

"I could kill you."

"You are."

"How can you resist me?"

"It isn't easy. Luckily, you're a sick woman."

"Horse manure," Renée said. "Tell me how pretty I am."

I looked at her lying there. "You look like a perfect biological specimen. Everything's in the right place, the titties are pointing in the right direction, but a little saggy because you're flat out like that. The snatch is cute, very decorous, but for a connoisseur like me, maybe a little bushy. A touch with a pair of scissors might sharpen up the angles and trim it down to size. . . ."

"Oh, you dirty . . ."

"Ah-ah . . . you're a sick woman, remember?" I held up my hand to stop her. "But you look kissable and parts of you are wet and inviting and if I didn't have all the moral turpitude I was born with, do you know what I'd do?"

"I wish you'd just screw me and shut up."

"You got no class, Renée."

"You got no dick, Mike Hammer."

"Want references?" I asked her. "How's the head?"

She touched her scalp with her fingertips and winced. "Sore, but not that sore. I've been deliberately taking advantage of my . . . condition, and staying bedridden."

"I know. And your boss is up in the air over your disappearance. It seems that he can't get along without you. I'm here on a rescue mission to get you back to work."

Her mouth formed a fake pout. "I thought you just wanted to see me."

"Right now I'm seeing all of you there is to see."

"You've missed the other side."

"Leave something to the imagination, will you? Besides, suppose that maid of yours walks in here?"

"Oh, she'll understand."

I shook my head and laughed. Dames. "Get up and get

125

dressed. If you hustle I'll have a coffee with you while I use your phone."

Renée grimaced and tossed a pillow at me. "Your casual treatment is making me feel married, you big slob. How can you resist me like this?"

"It isn't easy at all, sugar. If I had the time I'd tear you apart."

"Nothing but promises."

I threw the pillow back at her and went back to the living room. The chubby little maid with the odd accent had her coat on and asked me to tell Miss Talmage she was leaving for the afternoon, but would be back around five to prepare supper. If she was needed, she could be reached at her sister's. Miss Talmage had the number.

When she left I picked up the phone and called Henaghan at the New York City Department of Public Works. His second secretary found him and put him through.

"Hey, Mike," he yelled. "What's new?"

"Need some information, Henny."

"Well, this is a public department."

"See if you can check and find out what construction units have been issued permits for blasting inside the city limits. Can do?"

There was a small silence and Henaghan said, "Aw, Mike, have you taken a look around lately? This town is like a beehive. They're putting up stuff all over the place."

"Yeah, but they only blast during the ground operation. It shouldn't be all that difficult."

"Look, I'll give you a number . . ."

"No dice. I'll get handed from file clerks to petty officials who'll want explanations and authorizations and still come up with year-old information. I could do better touring the city in a taxi taking notes and I haven't got that much time. You do it for me."

"Mike . . ." Henny sounded harried.

"Or do you forget me having to run up to Albany to get you out of the can last summer? Or that time in Miami when . . ."

"Okay, okay. Don't remind me. The memories are too painful. Where are you?"

I gave him the phone number.

"Stay there. It may take a little while, but I'll expedite things."

From the bedroom I heard the shower cut off and clothes hangers rattling in a closet. I stared absently at the rain slashing against the window and picked up the phone again, dialed my office number and activated the tape recorder.

And Velda had finally called in. Her voice was crisp and hurried, no words wasted at all. She said, "Suspect located at Anton Virelli's area and running fast. Ballinger's right behind him with his men but haven't pinpointed his location. If you haven't hit it yet, suspect goes by name of Beaver and knows he's being tracked. He's been working his way uptown and has something on his mind, probably a safe place to hide out. He should be making a move soon if he sticks to his timetable. My guess is he'll come out of the west end of the block so I'm going to take a chance and cover the Broadway side. I'll call back as soon as he shows."

That was the end of the message and I was about to hang up when another click signaled a further message and a voice said, "Uh, Mike? Like this is you or a machine. Mike?" There was a pause, then, "So you're automated. Everything's gone automated." I felt like telling that silly Caesar Mario Tulley to hurry up and get with it, but you don't rush the new generation. "You know how you was asking about that guy in the red vest? So I split a joint with an old friend and we get to talking and I asked and sure enough, he knows a guy who knows him. I'm going to see him later, so if you get down this way I'll be working around the Winter Garden. Maybe I'll have something for you. Uh . . . how the hell do you say so long to a machine anyway?" He mumbled something else and the connection was ended.

Damn, it was closing in fast. The ends were beginning to meet, but they were all tied up inside a tape recorder and I had to wait for the spool to roll. But Velda had narrowed it down somewhat. Anton Virelli was a bookie who operated from a storefront on Ninety-second Street just off Broadway. At least now I knew what area to concentrate on. I called Pat and rousted him out of bed at home. He hadn't had much sleep, but he softened the growl in his voice and listened when I gave him the information. He thought he could tap a couple of plainclothesmen to probe the area for Beaver and he could get a warrant out for Woody and his boys that might slow them down long enough for us to reach our man first. I thanked him and hung up.

A lovely voice behind me said, "Beaver. What an odd name. The people you know."

I turned around and Renée was standing there, fresh from the shower, her hair piled on top of her head,

127

wrapped in a heavy white terry-cloth robe belted tightly enough to make her a living hourglass. She smelled of summery fragrances and bath oils and she pirouetted gracefully so I could see all of her, then wrinkled her nose at me, brought in a tray with a coffee pot and two cups and sat down.

"Great," she said. "Naked, I get no reaction. Completely covered in an old robe you simper like a kid. What's with you men?"

I took the coffee she handed me. "We like the mystery better."

"Liar. Business is more important to you. What have you been so busy about and who is Beaver? Another one of your friends who shoot at people?"

"I never met the guy."

She gave me a hurt look. "All right, you don't have to tell me anything. But don't blame me for being curious, please. After all, I did get shot and it was a new experience, one that I wouldn't like to repeat, and I thought some kind of explanation might be in order."

Wind from the river rattled the window and the rain tried to claw its way in. I looked at her and grinned. Hell, she was entitled. I fished in my pocket and took out the three photos of Beaver, handing her one. I let her look at it while I started from the beginning and brought her up to date. But it was really me I was talking to, trying to jell the details in my mind, picking out the strange little flaws and attempting to force in things that didn't belong or should have.

She handed the picture back and I stuck it in my pocket.

The phone still sat there, impassive and unconcerned with it all.

The muscles were tight across my back and my hands were knotted into balls of rage.

"Mike ..." she came over to me and unbuttoned my jacket, then slipped it off, her hands kneading the back of my neck. I closed my eyes and felt the tension begin to melt under the gentle pressure of her fingers. She tugged the shoulder harness off then and let the .45 drop to the floor, then it was my tie and my shirt, her hands working their way across my chest and arms. Her palms pushed me back on the couch and her fingers worked at my belt and I just let her go ahead until she was done. I felt her stand up, heard the soft whisper of cloth and let my eyes slit open a bare fraction and watched her standing there warmly nude and smiling. "Don't move," she said.

128

I closed my eyes again, wiping out all thought for the minute she was gone, then heard her come in and opened them again. She threw a pillow on the floor beside the couch, knelt down with her arms outstretched and the vibrator she had attached to her hand started to pulsate crazily as she started at my neck and began a slow, deliberate journey into other areas.

Time went by in slow, lazy circles, then the erotic tingling of the vibrator stopped and a more intense sensation replaced it until time erupted into an explosive spiral that diminished out of sight and left me gasping for breath.

On the table the phone had come to life.

I opened my eyes and Renée said, "Good?"

"Beautiful."

I reached over and picked up the receiver.

Henaghan told me I probably could have done better with the taxi ride, but came up with five places conducting blasting operations at the moment. I wrote them all down, thanked him and hung up, looking at the list in my hand.

Only one place was above Fifty-Second Street, an area off Columbus Avenue at One Hundred-tenth Street. And that wasn't anywhere near Anton Virelli's territory at all. If Velda was holding down a stakeout around Ninety-second and Broadway, she was doing it alone. Somehow Beaver had cut loose earlier and with more manpower to cover the exits, Woody and his boys had caught his move and had him cornered in another location.

In a way it was a relief to me. She was out of the action now and I wanted to keep it that way. If Velda didn't tumble to the fact that Beaver was gone I could move in alone without sweating about her catching a slug. I looked at the paper again and swore softly. An area, that's all it was. A big flat area with hundreds of holes to crawl into. Those blasting signals were clear, but distant, tonal enough to penetrate phone booth walls or old apartments. There wasn't any chance of tracking down every telephone in the neighborhood at all. What I needed was an address. Beaver was heading for one definite spot, that was sure. One place where he figured he'd be safe. He was enough of an old hand to stay out of the hands of other pros so far and he'd be playing it smart and cagy.

Caesar Mario Tulley was going to get me that address.

Renée had slipped back into her robe and was sitting on the end of the couch, watching me with a small, wistful smile. "I hate telephones," she said.

"Things are beginning to move."

"I know. You came, now you have to go."

"Your turn the next time," I said.

"It's all right, Mike. Some things are more important than others." She saw me frowning, not knowing how to answer her, and nodded. "Really, I understand," she added.

"Beaver's someplace around Columbus and a Hundred-tenth Street, Woody's boys have him hemmed in. He's probably pinned down temporarily, but not located yet. I want first crack at that bastard."

"You know where he is?"

"No, but somebody else might have the answer."

"Mike ..." Renée's face went soft and worried. "Please be careful. I would like to see you again."

"You will."

"This wild business of yours ... well, I guess I've been in a pretty distant world." She licked her lips and shook her head in disbelief. "Dead people ... I've been shot ..." her eyes met mine then, " ... and you, Mike."

"Things aren't all that bad," I said.

She tried to smile, but it was forced. I suddenly felt pretty silly standing there without any clothes on. She knew what I was feeling, faked a grin, then stood up and frowned. Her hand shot out to the table to support herself.

"You all right?" I asked her.

She touched the side of her head, blinked, then nodded, taking a deep breath. "Just my head. I still can't move too quickly. I get dizzy when I do." Her smile came back, this time with natural ease. "Why don't you go inside and get dressed? I'm going to call my maid back. There are times when I just don't like to be left alone."

I picked up my clothes, somehow feeling guilty, and went into the bedroom. I showered quickly, climbed into my clothes, snugged the .45 down in its sling and went back into the living room.

For a minute I thought she wasn't there, then I saw a small upturned palm sticking out from behind the chair and half ran to where she was lying. Her eyes were partially slitted open and a trickle of blood was oozing down from under the pad on her scalp.

I got my hands under her arms and lifted her to the couch, stretching her out with a pillow under her feet. A couple of ice-cold wet towels finally brought a flicker to her eyes and she moaned softly. "What the hell happened, kid?"

She let her eyelids close, then open. "I was ... calling

Maria . . . and I fainted." I looked at the compress on her head. One end had come loose from where it had evidently hit something. She winced and pushed my hand away.

"You want me to get a doctor?"

"No . . . I'll be all right. Please . . . don't leave until Maria gets here."

"Sure, kid. How do you feel?"

"Awful . . . headache."

Luckily, Maria's sister only worked three blocks away and she was there in ten minutes. She helped me get Renée into bed, but kept looking at me suspiciously as though she didn't believe what really had happened. She made me leave while she got a nightgown on her, then came bustling back into the living room, frowning. Just in time I kicked the vibrator under the couch before she saw it. "You stay. I'm going to the drugstore for something to make her sleep."

I got that guilty feeling again and just nodded.

From the bedroom I heard Renée call my name and I walked in and took her hand. There was a fresh bandage in place and the blood had been wiped from her hair. "Mike .. I'm sorry."

"Forget it."

"Go do what you have to do," she said softly.

I looked at my watch. It was still early. Caesar liked to work the later crowds; he looked a little more pitiful under the night lights. "I got time," I told her.

It was thirty minutes before Maria got back with a plastic, bottle of capsules, and another thirty before the drowsiness came over Renée's eyes. Just before they closed, she said, "It *was* nice, wasn't it, Mike?"

"Crazy, but beautiful," I answered.

Maria gave me another of those stern looks and nodded toward the door. "Now you go."

And I went.

I called William Dorn's apartment from the first open bar I came to. A maid answered and said Mr. Dorn was in a business conference and couldn't be disturbed at the moment.

"Give him a message for me, please."

"Certainly, sir."

"Tell him Miss Talmage suffered a slight relapse and has been given a sedative, but there's nothing to worry about."

"Oh . . . then she won't be at the meeting this evening?"

"I'm afraid not."

131

"Yes, thank you, Doctor. Is there anything Mr. Dorn can do?"

"Nothing at all."

"Very well, Doctor, and thank you again."

I hung up and grunted. I didn't think I sounded like a doctor at all.

The rain was coming down harder and I turned up my collar against it. Somewhere Beaver was hiding and Woody and his boys were waiting.

It was going to be a trouble night.

CHAPTER 10

They could only hold the story back just so long. When more than one person knows, there is no secret. The final edition of the evening paper carried the opener that was the crack in the whole faulty scheme of security. An unmentioned source had leaked the information that the dead guy in the subway station had died of a highly contagious disease and upon further investigation nothing could be learned from officialdom about the matter. There were vigorous denials, but no one offered another explanation. The Newark paper went a little further, an editorial demanding an answer over a body-shot of the corpse.

So far nobody had put the obvious pieces in place . . . the sudden show of harmony between the U.S. and the U.S.S.R., the burst of activity from the armed forces reservists and the presence of the Fort Detrick C.B. warfare teams. But it was coming. No amount of security was going to stop people with imagination from thinking along certain lines, then proving out their theories. Tomorrow a few more questions would be asked, then when no answers were forthcoming the dam would burst and every end of the news media would be jamming down the throat of bureaucracy. Tom-Tom Schneider was dead, his killers were dead. What other pieces of sensationalism could they dig up to bury the biggest news story of them all?

I walked up Broadway past the offices of WOBY–TV and wondered how Eddie Dandy was doing. On impulse, I turned in out of the wet, found the receptionist just going out for a coffee break and asked her.

Eddie Dandy had just come in an hour ago. He was in his office and wasn't to be disturbed. I thanked her, let her go for her coffee and took the elevator upstairs. I spotted the two guys by his door before they saw me, turned right instead of toward his office, rounded the corridor until I found an empty desk and picked up the phone and dialed Eddie's number.

His hello was tired and curt and I said, "Mike Hammer, Ed. How goes it?"

"Stinking, kid. Where are you?"

"Right down the hall. Can you break away from the watchdogs long enough to go to the john?"

"Yeah, sure, but look, buddy ... I'm strictly off limits. Anybody caught talking to me gets the same solitary confinement treatment."

"Balls."

"Man, they did it to me."

"I'm not you. Give me five minutes, then cut out."

The men's room was across the corridor, out of sight from the pair, and I went in without being seen. Nobody else was there, so I stepped into the end booth and closed the door. Five minutes later I heard the outside door hiss shut and walked out of the cubicle.

Eddie looked tired, but his eyes were bright and his mouth tight with constrained rage. "You look terrible," I said.

His eyes went toward the door. "Quiet. They're standing outside."

"How'd you shake loose? I thought they had you under wraps."

"A few nosy buddies of mine started poking around when I didn't show. The big wheels figured I'd be better off where I could be seen and answer monitored phone calls that could be chopped off fast if I started to squawk. Brother, when this is over asses are going to burn, and I mean burn."

"It isn't over yet," I reminded him.

His face turned gray and he seemed ten years older. "I was in on some high level discussion, Mike. You really know how bad it is?"

"Maybe I'm better off not knowing."

Eddie didn't even hear me. "There's no place to hide. Everybody would be running for cover, but *there's no place to hide!* They've isolated that damned disease and it's the worst thing they ever came up against. Once it gets started there's no stopping it, no vaccines, no natural barriers ... nothing. The damn stuff is so self-perpetuating it can even feed on itself after it's done feeding on everything else. Maybe a few guys will escape it for a while. The men in the Antarctic on Operation Deepfreeze will miss it because intense cold is the only thing that can stop it, but where will they be when the supply planes stop coming in?"

"Eddie ..."

134

"Hell, for years they talked about the atom bomb, the big boom that could wipe out the world. They should have talked about something else. At least that would have been quick. This makes nuclear fission look like a toy."

"There's still a chance."

"Not much, friend. Only one guy knew where those containers were planted and now he's dead."

I shrugged and looked at him. "So what's left to do?"

He finally broke a grin loose and waved his arms in mock disgust at me. "I wish I could think like you, Mike. No kidding, I really do. I'd go out, find a few broads and start banging away until it was all over. Me, I'm just going to sit and sweat and swear and worry until my time comes to check out, then maybe I'll cry a little, get drunk as hell and not have to fight a hangover."

"Pessimists are a pain in the butt," I said.

"You're absolutely nuts, Mike. How can you stand there and . . ."

"I have my own business to take care of."

Eddie let out a grunt of disbelief. "Still Lippy Sullivan? Just like things weren't . . ."

"It keeps me busy," I interrupted. I brought him up to date and by the time I was done he had almost forgotten about what was happening outside.

"Woody Ballinger's a rough boy to snag in a trap, Mike. He's been around. If that dip lifted something from his wallet and tried to shake him down for it, he was plain asking to be killed. You ought to let Woody do you a favor and knock him off."

"Not this guy. As long as we still have murder one punishment, I want him to go through the whole damn torturous process."

"So what can I do?"

I looked at my watch again. Time was going by fast. Outside, darkness had blacked out a wet city and the rain was still scratching against the windows. "Do me a favor," I said. "Get a call through to Pat Chambers for me and tell him to drop the area around Ninety-second and get his men over to Columbus and One Hundred-tenth. If they spot Velda, don't tip her to the move. Can you do that?"

"Sure. Those kind of calls I can make, so long as I stay off the Big Subject."

"They letting you broadcast?"

"Nothing live. I have to tape it first. They thought of everything."

I looked around the room and grinned. "Except this."

"Yeah. Who makes appointments in men's rooms except sexual deviates?"

"Don't let it get around. That might make more news."

Suddenly his eyes clouded. "Wait until tomorrow. They really got a beaut cooked up. The public will flip, Wall Street stocks will tumble and the news outlets will eat it up. There won't be room enough in any paper or broadcast for anything else."

"Oh? Why?"

"The President is scheduled to have a serious heart attack," he said.

Caesar Mario Tulley hadn't shown up and nobody had seen him around since earlier in the day. Little Joe had taken up his usual rainy night station in the back booth of Aspen's Snack Bar, peering out the window, sipping one coffee after another.

He shrugged when I asked him and said, "Don't worry about him, Mike. He'll show. A night like this, the kid makes out, all wet and sorry-looking. Wish I could make half of his take. The suckers feel worse over a long-haired kid in dirty clothes panhandling nickels than a guy like me with no legs."

"Quit complaining," I said. "You got it made."

Little Joe laughed and took another sip of his coffee. "If I didn't I wouldn't be inside. Man, I had my times out there on nights like this. It was good hustling, but hell on the health. You look for him over at Leo's?"

"They didn't see him."

"How about Tessie . . . you know, Theresa Miller, that cute little whore from the Village. She never stops. If there's a live one on the street she'll tap him."

"She saw him this afternoon, not since," I said. "Look, he told me he was going to see a friend. You know who he hangs out with?"

"Come on, Mike. Them hippies all look alike to me. Sure, I seen him with a few creeps before, but nobody I could finger. Hell, I don't even want to get close to 'em. He works his side of the street, I work mine. Look, why don't you try Austin Towers? Tall, lanky guy with a scraggly goatee. Always hangs out by the paper kiosk the next block down. He sells them kids pot and if anybody would know, he would."

I told Little Joe thanks and flipped him a five-spot.

He grabbed it and grinned. "I never refuse money," he said.

Austin Towers didn't want to talk, but he thought it was

a bust and didn't have time to dump the two paper bags he had in his raincoat pocket and gave me a resigned look and followed me into the semilit entrance of the closed shoe store.

"I want to talk to a lawyer," he said.

All I did was look at him.

For a second he stared back, then dropped his eyes nervously and a tic pulled at the corner of his mouth.

I still didn't say anything.

"Listen, Mister . . ."

I let him see the .45 under my coat and his eyes widened and he tried to swallow the lump in his throat. His voice was a hoarse whisper when he said, "Man, look, look . . . I'm just pushing grass. I ain't crowding nobody. I don't hold no hard stuff, not me. Man, it's all grass and who puts heat on grass? You guys want me out, I go pick another spot and . . ."

"Where can I find Caesar?"

The relief that flooded his face swept over him like a wave. "Oh, man, he ain't nothin', that guy. He just . . ."

"You see him today?"

"Sure, about four. He bought some stuff so he and a friend . . ."

He was talking fast and furiously, happy to know it wasn't him I was leaning on. I cut him short. "Where is he?"

"His pal got a pad on Forty-ninth. First floor over the grocery in the front."

"Show me."

"Mister . . ."

I didn't want him making any phone calls that would scare off my birds. "Show me," I said again.

And he showed me. A stinking, miserable two-room flop that reeked of garbage and marijuana smoke where Caesar Mario Tulley and a scruffy-looking jerk in shoulder-length hair were wrapped in Mexican serapes, stretched out on the floor completely out of their skulls from the pot party.

I said, "Damn!" and the word seemed to drop in the room like soft thunder.

Austin Towers started edging toward the door. "Like I showed you, man, so now I gotta cut, y'know?"

"Get back here, freak."

"Man . . ."

"Killing you would be a public service." My voice had such an edge to it that he scurried back like a scared rat, his head bobbing, eager to do anything that would keep him alive. "How long are they going to be out of it?"

"How would I know, man?"

I snapped my head around and stared at him, watching his breath catch in his chest. "You sold him the stuff. You know how much they had. Now check them to see what's left and make a guess and make a good one or I'll snap your damn arms in half."

He didn't argue about it. One look at my face and he knew I wasn't kidding. He bent over the pair, patted them down expertly, finding the remnants of the joints they had gone through, then stood up. "Used it all. Man, they tied one on, them two. Maybe three-four hours you might reach 'em if you're lucky."

This time I grinned, my lips pulled tight across my teeth. "Maybe if *you're* lucky it'll be one hour. One. You're in the business, boy, so you'd better know all the tricks. You start working on them and don't stop until they're awake. Don't bother trying to run out. You couldn't run fast or far enough that I couldn't nail you, so play it sweet and cool and you might get out of this in one piece. One hour, kid. Get them back and I don't give a damn how you do it."

"Man, you don't know this stuff!" His voice was nearly hysterical.

"No, but you do," I told him.

Velda had called in again. She was still on the stakeout but getting edgy because there had been no tip-off to Beaver's whereabouts. She was going to give it one more hour and then try another possible lead. That left me forty-six minutes to work ahead of her.

The taxi dropped me at the corner of Columbus Avenue and a Hundred-tenth Street and when I looked around the memories of the old days from when I was a kid came rushing back like an incoming tide. There were changes, but some things never change at all. The uneven rooftops still were castle battlements, each street a gateway in the great wall. The shufflers still shuffled, oblivious to the weather, urchin noises and cooking smells mingling in this vast stomach of a neighborhood. Plate glass windows protected with steel grilling, others unconcernedly dark and empty. The perennial tavern yellow-lit behind streaked glazing, the drugstore still sporting the huge red and purple urns, the insignia of its trade. On a good night the young bloods would be gathered on the corners, swapping lies and insults, protecting their turf. The hookers would cruise for their johns and the pushers would be clearing the path to an early grave for the users.

They didn't know me here, but they knew I wasn't an outsider. I was born part of the scene and still looked it and they didn't mind me asking things and didn't mind answering. I showed the photo of Beaver to the bartender in Steve's Bar and Grill. He didn't know the guy, but took it to the back room and showed it to somebody else. One guy thought he looked familiar, but that was all.

In the candy store, the old man shook his head and told me the man in the picture looked like somebody good to stay away from and tried to talk about the old days until I thanked him and went back outside.

A gypsy cab driver having coffee and a doughnut in his car scanned the photo and said he was pretty sure he had seen the guy around, but didn't know where or when. It was the eyes, he said. He always looked at people's eyes, and he remembered seeing him. He told me to look for Jackie, the redheaded whore who swore she was a prostitute because she wanted money to go to college. Jackie knew everybody.

Jackie knew Beaver, all right. He had bought her pitch about two weeks ago, gone to her apartment and parted with ten bucks for sexual services rendered, leaving her with a few welts and bruises. She had seen him once after that, getting into a taxi down the block. She knew he didn't live in the area, but assumed he dropped up to see a friend who did. No, she couldn't even guess at who it was. The neighborhood was full of itinerants and strange faces. She took my ten bucks and thought I was a nut for not getting the whole go for the money.

Now, at least, I was in the area.

There were three construction sites within two blocks. One was a partial demolition job and the other two were leveled. The last one had wiped out a row of three brownstones all the way to the corner and the cut went deep into the solid rock that was the bed of the city. The hole was spotted with small ponds of rainwater and a yellow backhoe tractor stood lonely and dead-looking in the middle of the gorge, its toothed claw ready to pounce into the granite, but dead, like a suddenly frozen prehistoric beast.

Silent air compressors and equipment shacks lined one side of the street, abutted on either end by battered dump trucks. A square patch of dim light outlined the window of the watchman's stubby trailer and from behind the locked door I could hear Spanish music working toward a finale of marimbas and bongo drums before the announcer came on to introduce the next number.

I knocked on the door and it opened to a toothy grin and a stale beer smell and the young-old guy standing there said, "Come in, come in. Don't stand in the rain."

"Thanks." I stepped inside while he turned down the radio.

"Not much of a place," he said, "but I like it."

"Why not?"

"Sure, why not? It's a living. I got my own house and nobody to bitch at me. Pretty damn noisy in the daytime, then I got so I could sleep through anything. Maybe that's why they keep me on. Me, I can stay awake all night and sleep daytimes like they want. Don't get much company, though. Now, what can I do for you?"

I showed him the picture of Beaver and let him study it. "Ever see that man?"

He looked at it intently, then handed it back. "Can't say. Daytimes I sleep, y'know. After a while them damn compressors get to be like music and they put me right to sleep. Know something? I got so's I can't sleep without 'em going."

"You're sure?" I asked.

He nodded. "Don't remember him. We've been here a month already and I don't remember him. Know most everybody else, though. Especially the kids. The ones who like to climb all over things."

I was about to leave when I turned around and looked at him. "The crew work in the rain?"

"Hell no! They finished up right after it started and shut everything down. Them boys got the life, they have. Busted up my sleep real awful. When the compressors went off, I woke up. Shit, feller, I haven't been able to get back to sleep since. Everything's just too damn quiet. Look, you want a beer?"

"No thanks."

"You a cop? Maybe for the company?"

"Private investigator."

"Oh, about that stuff the kids took last week. Hell, we got it all back before they could hock it."

"You been cooped up here all day?"

"Naw, I walked around some. Didn't leave the block, though. Just bought some grub and beer, walked around to stretch out. Never leave the place alone long, and never at night. That's why they keep me on."

I pulled up a folding chair with my toe and hooked my leg over it. "See any strange faces around at all?"

140

"Ah, you got bums comin' through all the time. They go from . . ."

"Not bums. These wouldn't be bums."

"Who'd come down this way if they wasn't bums? Maybe some kids from . . . hey . . . yeah, wait a minute. When I went for the beer . . . before it got dark."

"So?"

"I see this car go by twice. New job with two guys in the front seat. It stopped halfway up on the other side and one got out. Then the car went up further and parked. I really didn't pay no attention to it on accounta it was raining so hard. When I came back the car was gone."

"A late-model, black, four-door job?"

"Yeah, how'd you know?"

"It's parked up on Columbus outside the drugstore," I said. "You got a phone here?"

"Under the blankets on the cot there. I like to keep it muffled. Can't stand them damn bell noises."

Pat wasn't in, but I got hold of Sergeant Corbett and told him to get a message through and gave him my location. He told me Pat had assigned an unmarked cruiser to the area earlier, but they were being pulled out in another thirty minutes. Too much was happening to restrict even one car team in a quiet zone on a quiet night and I was lucky to get the cooperation I did.

I said, "It may not be so damn quiet in a little while, buddy."

"Well, it won't be like the U.N. or the embassy joints. Everybody's in emergency sessions. You'll still be lucky if you get thirty minutes."

I hung up and tossed the covers back over the phone. The watchman was bent over the radio again with a beer in his hand, reading a comic book lying open on the floor.

My watch said Velda had left her post fifteen minutes ago. Somehow, someway, she'd find a thread, then a string, then a rope that would draw her right to this block.

I went out, closed the door and looked up the street, then started to walk slowly. On half the four-floor tenements were white square cardboard signs lettered in black notifying the world that the building was unfit for tenancy or scheduled for demolition. The windows were broken and dark, the fronts grime-caked and eroded. One building was occupied despite the sign, either by squatters with kerosene lamps or some undaunted tenant fighting City Hall. In the middle of the block was one brownstone, the basement renovated years ago into a decrepit tailor shop no wider than a big closet. A tilted sign on the door said a forlorn OPEN, and I would have passed it up entirely if I hadn't seen the dot of light through the crack in the drawn blind.

Sigmund Katz looked like a little gnome perched on his stool, methodically handstitching a child's coat, glasses on the end of his nose, bald head shiny under the single low-watt bulb. His eyes through the thick glasses were blue and watery, his smile weak, but friendly. An old-world accent was thick in his voice when he spoke. "No, this man in the picture I did not see," he told me.

"And you know everyone?"

"I have been here sixty-one years, young man." He paused and looked up from his needlework. "This is the only one you are looking for?" There was an expression of patient waiting on his face.

"There could be others."

"I see. And these are . . . not nice people?"

"Very bad people, Mr. Katz."

"They did not look so bad," he said.

"Who?"

"They were young and well dressed, but it is not in the appearance that makes a person good or bad, true?"

I didn't want to push him. "True," I said.

"One used the phone twice. The second time the other one stopped him before he could talk. I may not see too well, but my hearing is most good. There were violent words spoken."

I described Carl and Sammy and he nodded.

"Yes," he said, "those are the two young men."

"When they left here . . . did you see where they went?"

The old man smiled, shook his head gently and continued sewing. "No, I'm afraid I didn't. Long ago I learned never to interfere."

I unclenched the knots my fingers were balled into and took a deep breath. *Time, damn it, it was running out!*

Before I could leave he added, "However, there was Mrs. Luden for whom I am making this coat for her grandson. She thought they were salesmen, but who would try to sell in this poor neighborhood? Not well dressed young men who arrive in a shiny new car. They knock on doors and are very polite."

I watched him, waiting, trying to stay relaxed.

"Perhaps they did find a customer. Not so long ago they went into Mrs. Stone's building across the street where the steps are broken and haven't come out."

The tension leaked out of my muscles like rain from my hair and I grinned humorously at Mr. Katz.

His eyes peered at me over his glasses. "Tell me, young man, you look like one thing, but you may be another. By one's appearance, you cannot tell. Are you a nice man?"

"I'm not one of *them*."

"Ah, but are you a nice man?"

"Maybe to some people," I said.

"That is good enough. Then I tell you something else. In Mrs. Stone's building ... there are not just two men. Three went up the first time, then a few minutes ago, another two. Be careful, young man. It is not good."

And now things were beginning to shape up!

I ran back into the rain and the night, cut across the street and found the building with the broken steps, took them two at a time on the side that still held and unsheathed the .45 and thumbed the hammer back. The front door was partially ajar and I slammed it open with the flat of my hand and tried to see into the inkwell of the vestibule. It took seconds for my eyes to adjust, then I spotted the staircase and started toward it.

And time ran out.

From a couple of floors up was a crash of splintering wood, a hoarse yell and the dull blast of heavy caliber guns in rapid fire, punctuated by the flatter pops of lighter ones. Somebody screamed in wild agony and a single curse ripped through the musty air. I didn't bother trying to be quiet. I took the steps two at a time and almost made the top when I saw the melee at the top lit momentarily in the burst of gunfire, then one figure burst through the others and came smashing down on top of me in a welter of arms and legs, gurgling wetly with those strange final sounds of death, and we both went backward down the staircase into an old cast iron radiator with sharp edges that bit into my skull in a blinding welter of pain and light.

CHAPTER 11

Velda was crying through some distant rage. I heard her say, "Damn it, Mike, you're all right! You're all right! Mike . . . answer me!"

My head felt like it was split wide open and I felt myself gag and almost threw up. The light from Velda's flash whipped into my eyes, beating at my brain like a club for a second until I pushed it away.

"Mike . . .?"

"I'm not shot," I said flatly.

"Damn you, why didn't you wait? Why didn't you call . . ."

"Ease off." I pushed to my knees and took the flash from her and turned it on the body. There was a bloody froth around the mouth and the eyes were glassy and staring. Sammy had bought his farm too.

Across the street people were shouting and a siren had started to whine. I let Velda help me up, then groped my way up the stairs to the top. The President wouldn't have to have a heart attack after this. The pictures would take care of all the gory news the public was interested in. Carl was sprawled out face down on the kitchen floor of the apartment with half his head blown away, a skinny little guy in a plaid sports coat and dirty jeans was tied to a chair with a hole in his chest big enough to throw a cat through, his toupee flopping over one ear. Like the little whore had told me, one was partially bald. Woody Ballinger was in a curiously lifelike position of being asleep with his head on an overturned garbage sack, one hand over his heart like a patriotic citizen watching the flag go by. Only his hand covered a gaping wound that was all bright red and runny.

That was all.

Beaver wasn't there.

I walked over and looked at the broken chair beside the table with the ropes in loose coils around the remnants.

144

Somebody else had been tied up too. Behind the chair was a broken window leading to the rear fire escape and on one of the shards of glass was a neat little triangle of red wool. The kind they make vests out of.

The flash picked out an unbroken bulb and I snapped it on. In the dull light it looked even messier and Velda made heaving noises in her throat.

I looked at the table top and knew why Woody wanted Beaver so badly. His policy code sequence identifying the workings of his organization was laid out there on a single sheet of typewritten paper that had been folded so that it would fit a pocket wallet.

And that was why Woody wanted Beaver. But who had wanted Woody?

My head felt like it wanted to burst. In a minute the place would be crawling with cops. And outside, there still was Beaver, and *I wanted him.*

I shoved the unfired .45 back in the sling and turned to Velda. "You stay here and handle it, kitten. Give them as much as you know, but give me running time."

"Mike . . ."

"This was only one stop on Beaver's route. He's heading someplace else." I went over to the window and put one leg through. "How did you know about this place?"

"One of Anton Virelli's runners saw Woody's car here. He reported in."

"You see anybody leave the building?"

"I'm . . . not sure. I was looking for you."

"Okay, sugar. Stall 'em. They're coming up."

Austin Towers had had more than the hour he expected and he hadn't wasted any of it. Caesar and his friend were sitting up, shivering under cold wet sheets, trying to keep their feet off the sodden rug on the floor. The dull luster was still in their eyes, but they were awake enough to mumble complaints at Towers who threatened them with another bucket of ice water if they tried to get up.

When he heard me come in he almost dropped the pail and stood stiff in his tracks, waiting to see if I approved or not. Caesar let his head sag toward me and managed a sick grin. "Hi, Mike. Get . . . get this bastard . . . outa here."

"Shut up, punk." I took the pail from Towers and sat it on the floor. "How good are they?"

"Man, I tried. Honest . . ."

"Can they think coherently?"

"Yeah, I'd say so. It ain't exactly like a booze hang-over. They . . ."

"Okay then, cut out." He started to move around me and I grabbed his arm. Very slowly I brought the .45 up where he could see it. His face went pasty white and his knees started to sag. "This is the kind of trouble that stuff brings. You're not invulnerable ... and kid, you're sure expendable as hell. Start thinking twice before you peddle that crap again."

His head bobbed in a nod and new life came back into his legs. "Man," he said, "I'm thinking! I'm thinking right now."

I let him go. "Scram."

He didn't wait for me to repeat the invitation. He even left his coat on the back of the chair. Caesar chuckled and tried to unwrap himself from the sheet. "Thanks, old pal Mike. That guy ... he sure was bugging us. Gimme a hand. I'm freezing to death."

"In a minute." I glanced at the other guy, slack-lipped and bony, like a sparrow under the wet cloth. "This the guy you were going to meet about Beaver?"

"Sure, Mike." He let out a belch and moaned, his teeth chattering. "So we meet like I said."

"You were going to meet me too, Caesar."

His face tried to scowl. "Look, if you're going to be like that ..." He saw me pick up the pail. "Okay, okay. I'm sorry. It ain't the end of the world."

I almost felt like telling him right then.

"Hey, Mister." The other one looked like he was coming apart at the seams. "I did like Caesar asked. My friend, he told me where this guy ... the one in the red vest, where he flops."

"Where?"

He gulped and tried to look straight at me. "Take ... this sheet off, huh?"

I hated to waste the time, but I couldn't afford to put up with a stubborn idiot. I undid the knots Tower had twisted the ends into and yanked the wet cloth away and he stumbled out of his chair and reached for the coat Towers had left and pulled it tightly around him, still shivering.

"Where?" I repeated.

"Carmine said he seen him at the Stanton Hotel. They're on the same floor."

"He describe him?"

"Tall. Skinny. Like kind of a mean character. He ain't there all the time, but he hangs onto his pad."

"What else?"

"Always the red vest. Never took it off. Like it was

146

lucky or something." I started to leave, then: "Mister ..."

"Yeah?"

"You got a quarter? I'm flat."

I tossed five bucks on the chair. "Unwrap the idiot there and you can both blow your minds. Someday take a look in a mirror and see what's happening to you."

I picked up a cruising cab on Eighth Avenue and gave him the address of the Stanton. Before the turn of the century it had been an exclusive, well-appointed establishment catering to the wealthy idler who wanted privacy for his extramarital affairs, but time and changes in neighborhood patterns had turned it into a way station for transients and a semipermanent pad for those living on the fringes of society.

A fifteen-truck Army convoy was blocking traffic, white-helmeted M.P.'s diverting cars west, and the driver cut left, swearing at all the nonsense. "Like the damn war, y'know? You'd think we was being invaded. The way traffic is already they could hold them damn maneuvers someplace else."

"Maybe they hate the mayor," I said.

He growled in answer, swerved violently around a timid woman driver who was taking up a lane and a half and yanked the cab through a slot and made a right on Tenth Avenue. I looked at my watch. Five after ten. An hour and a half since the slaughter uptown. Enough time for Beaver to collect his gear and make another run.

I didn't wait for change. I threw a bill on the seat beside the driver and got out without bothering to close the door. Fingers of rain clawed at my face, wind-whipping the drenching spray around my legs. Inside the lobby of the Stanton clusters of men trying to look busy were staying away from the night. A uniformed patrolman, a walkie-talkie slung over his shoulder, finished checking the groups and pushed through the doors, looked up at the sky in disgust, then lowered his head against the wind and turned west.

I went in, cut across the lobby to the desk where a bored clerk with a cigarette drooping from the corner of his mouth was doing a crossword puzzle on the counter.

He didn't bother looking up. "No rooms," he said.

I flipped the puzzle to the floor and knocked the cigarette from his mouth with a backhanded swipe and his head snapped up with a mean snarl and he had his hand all cocked to swing when he saw my face and faded. "You got bad manners, friend."

"If you're looking for trouble . . ."

"I *am* trouble, kiddo." I let him look at me for another few seconds, then he dropped his eyes and wiped his mouth, not liking what he saw. I reached in my pocket for the photos of Beaver. There were two left. Someplace I had left one, but it didn't matter now.

The clerk had seen cards like those before, but cops carried them, and I got the eyes again because he had figured me first for one thing, now he was trying to make me for another and it didn't jell. I put the card on the counter facing him. "Recognize him?"

He didn't want to talk, but he didn't want to know what would happen if he didn't, either. Finally he nodded. "Room 417."

"There now?"

"Came in earlier. His face was swollen and he was all bloodied up. What'd he do?"

"Nothing that would interest you."

"Listen, Mac . . . we're trying to stay clean. This guy never gave us no fuss so why are you guys . . ."

I grabbed his arm. "What *guys?*"

"There was another one before. Another cop. He wanted him too."

"Cop?"

"Sure. He had one of these mug cards."

Pat might have made it. One of his squad just might have gotten a lead and run it down. Enough of them had copies of the photos and one way or another Beaver could be nailed.

"You see them come out?" I asked him.

"Naw. I don't watch them bums. You think I ain't got nothin' better to do?"

"Yeah, I don't think you have. Just one more thing . . . stay off that phone."

A swamper in filthy coveralls was oiling down the wooden steps, so I pushed the button beside the elevators instead of walking up. The ancient machinery creaked and whined, finally groaning to a halt. The door slid open and two drunks were arguing over a bottle until one behind them pushed through with a muttered curse, almost knocking them down. He looked familiar, but I had seen too many lineups with these characters playing lead roles, so any of them could be familiar. The other two guys that pushed their way through were Vance Solito and Jimmy Healey, a pair of the Marbletop bunch who ran floating crap games on the side. I shoved the two drunks out to do their arguing and punched the button for the fourth floor.

Outside 417 I stopped and put my ear to the door. No sound at all. I slid the .45 out, thumbed the hammer back and rapped hard, twice. Nobody answered and I did it again with the same result. Then I tried the knob. The door was locked, but with the kind of lock it only took a minute to open. When I had the latch released I stepped aside and shoved it open and stared into the darkness that was intermittently lit by the reflected glow from a blinking light on the street below.

I waited, listening, then stepped around the door opening inside, flipped the light switch on and hit the floor. Nothing happened. I stood up, put the .45 back and closed the door. Nothing was going to happen.

Beaver was lying spread-eagled on the floor wallowing in his own blood, as dead as he ever was going to be, his stomach slit open and a vicious hole in his chest where a knife thrust had laid open muscle and bone before it carved into his heart. There were other carefully planned cuts and slices too, but Beaver had never made a sound through the tape that covered his mouth. His face was lumpy, bruised from earlier blows, with nasty charred and blistered hollows pockmarking his neck from deliberate cigarette burns.

But this was different. Woody had taken care of the first assault, but he hadn't gotten around to killing him and when the break came Beaver had dumped himself out of his chair, broken loose and gone through the window while all the action was going on. But this was different.

No, this was the same. It had happened before to Lippy Sullivan.

I took my time and read all the signs. It finally made sense when I thought it out. Beaver's break wasn't as clean as he had figured. He had been tailed to his safe place, hurting bad and terrified as hell. And when the killer finally reached him he couldn't run again. He was supposed to talk. He was tied up, his mouth taped while the killer told him what he wanted and what he was going to do to him if he didn't talk and just to prove his point the killer made his initial slashes that would insure his talking.

Except Beaver didn't talk. He fainted. There were more of those nicely placed slices, delivered purposely so the pain would bring him out of the faint. But Beaver didn't come out of it ... there had been too much before it and he lay there mute and unconscious until the killer couldn't wait any more and made sure he'd never talk to anybody else either. And when he was done killing he had torn the room apart, piece by piece, bit by bit.

149

I followed the search pattern looking for anything that might have been missed, fingering through the torn bedding, reaching into places somebody already had reached into, feeling outside around the window ledges, going through the contents of the single dresser whose drawers were stacked, empty, along one wall.

Beaver wasn't a fashion plate. He only had two suits and two sport jackets. The pockets were turned inside out and the coat linings ripped off. On the floor of the closet was a bloodstained shirt and a crumpled red vest with more blood, stiff and dried, staining the fabric.

I took another twenty minutes to make sure there was nothing I had missed and finally sat down on the edge of the bed, lit up a cigarette and looked at the mutilated body of Beaver on the floor.

I said, "You weren't lucky this time, chum. That red vest didn't bring you any luck at all, did it?"

Then I started to grin slowly and got up and went back to the closet where the red vest lay in a crushed lump. It wasn't much. It was old and worn and it must have been expensive at one time because it still held its color. Beaver had thrown it there when he took off his bloodied clothes, hurting and not caring about his lucky charm. It was too carelessly tossed off and not much for the killer to search because it didn't even have pockets.

But it had been Beaver's lucky charm once and a place to hide all his luck, something that was always with him and safe.

I found where the hand stitching was around the lower left hand edge, picked at the thread and pulled it out of the fabric. The sheet of onionskin paper folded there slid out and I opened it, scanned it slowly, then went to the phone and gave the desk clerk Eddie Dandy's number.

He said he knew how he could give his watchdogs the slip, but if he did that was the end of him in broadcasting, in life, in anything. He had been given the word strongly and with no punches pulled. He wanted to know if it was worth it.

I told him it was.

CHAPTER 12

I let him vomit his supper out in the toilet bowl and waited until he had mopped his face with cold water and dried off. He came back in the bedroom, trying to avoid the mess on the floor, but his eyes kept drifting back to the corpse until he was white again. He finally upended one of the drawers and sat on it, his hands shaking.

"Relax," I said.

"Damn it, Mike, did you have to get my ass in a sling just to show me this?"

I took a drag on my cigarette and nodded. "That's right."

Very slowly his face came out of his hands, his eyes drifting up to mine, fear cutting little crinkles into the folds of skin at their edges. "You . . . did you . . ."

"No, I didn't kill him."

Bewilderment replaced the fear and he said nervously, "Who did?"

"I don't know."

"Shit."

I went and got him a glass of water, waited while he finished it, looking out the window at the glassy-wet tops of the buildings across the street. Down below a police cruiser went by slowly and turned north at the corner. "Quiet out," I said.

Behind me, Eddie said softly, "It'll be a lot quieter soon. Just a few more days. I don't know why I was worrying about coming here at all. What difference can it make?"

"It hasn't happened yet."

"No chance, Mike. No chance at all. Everybody knows it. I wasted all that time worrying and sweating when I could have been like you, calm as hell and not giving a damn about anything. Maybe I'm fortunate at that. In a few days when the lid comes off and the whole world knows that it's only a little while before it dies, everybody

151

else will go berserk and I'll be able to watch them and have an easy drink to kiss things good-bye." He let out a little laugh. "I only wish I could have been able to tell the whole story. They talk openly now. It doesn't seem to matter any more. You didn't know the Soviets ran down more of the story, did you?"

I shook my head and watched the rain come down, only half hearing what he said.

"That other regime ... they never thought the strain of bacteria was so virulent. It would be contained pretty much in this hemisphere and die out after a certain length of time. They made tests on involuntary subjects and decided that one out of ten would be immune, and the vaccine they had developed would protect those they wanted protected. It wasn't just two agents who were planted in this country. There were twenty-two of them, and each was supplied with enough vaccine to immunize a hundred more, all key people in major commercial and political positions who would be ready to run the country after the plague was done wiping out the populace. Oh, they could sit back and not give a damn, but there was one thing they never got to know. The vaccine was no damn good. It was only temporary. They'll last a month or two longer after the others have died, but they'll die harder because it is going to take longer. Only they're not going to know this because everyone involved in the project is dead and there's nobody to tell them. They were going to know when it happened, because the single unknown, the key man who was going to plant the stuff around the country, was the only one who knew who the others were and he was going to notify them so they could set all their grand plans into motion."

"Nice," I said.

"So he planted the stuff ... all those containers. My guess is he lucked out because of the vaccine he was injected with. There was a possibility it could do that. Funny, isn't it?"

"Why?"

"Because they have that organization all set up. They're ready to move in and set up another semislave state. The elite few get it all and the rest get the garbage. Not bad if you're one of the elite few and have the only guns around to back you up. It doesn't even make any difference if those agents were given the date or not. Either way they think they'll be ready to grab it all. It might screw up their timing, but that's about all. They move in, think they have it made, then all of a sudden it hits them too."

"It won't happen."

Eddie Dandy laughed again, a flat, sour laugh that ended in a sob. "Mike, you're mad."

I turned around and looked at him perched on the edge of the drawer, muscles tightened with near hysteria bunching in his jaw. I grinned at him, then picked up the phone. It was five minutes before they located Pat Chambers and I let him take me apart in sections before I said, "You should have gone with me, friend. It wouldn't have taken all this time."

"What are you talking about?"

"You can buy next year's calendar, Pat. You'll be able to use it."

For ten seconds there was a long silence on the other end of the line. He knew what I was talking about, and his voice came back with a tone of such absolute consternation that I barely heard him say, "Mike . . ."

"It was all wrapped up in Lippy Sullivan," I told him. "Handle this gently, Pat. And Pat . . . you'd better pass the word that the President doesn't have to have a heart attack tomorrow. There'll be plenty of news for everybody to chew on . . . and when you're passing the word, pass it high up where it counts and none of those eager lads with all that political ambition will be able to get their teeth in my ass for what's going to happen. Tell the thinkers to get a good story ready, because there's going to be the damndest cover-up happening tomorrow you ever saw in your life, and while it's happening I'm going to be walking around with a big grin, spitting in their eyes."

Before he could answer I told him where I was and hung up. Eddie Dandy was watching me like I had gone out of my mind. I handed him the sheet of onionskin paper.

"What's this?"

"The exact location of every one of those containers. You have the manpower already alerted and placed, the experts from Fort Detrick on hand to decontaminate them and the biggest scoop of your whole career. Too bad you'll never really be able to tell about it." I looked at him and felt my face pull into a nasty grin, "Or the rest of it."

I tried one more call, but my party wasn't at home, which confirmed what I already knew. I took the two last photos of Beaver out of my pocket, looked at them and threw them down beside the body. He didn't look like that any more.

Spud Henry didn't know how to say it, the white lies not

153

quite fitting his mouth. Finally he said, "Oh, hell, Mikey boy, it's just that I got orders. He gimme special orders on the house phone. Nobody goes up. It's an important business meeting."

"How many are up there?"

"Maybe six."

"When'd the last one come in?"

"Oh, an hour ago. It was then I got the call. Nobody else."

"Look, Spud . . ."

"Mike, it won't make no difference. They got the elevator locked up on that floor and there ain't no other way. All the elevators stop the next floor down. There's a fire door, but it only opens from the inside and you can't even walk up. Come on, Mike, forget it."

"Sorry, Spud."

"Buddy, it's my job you got in your hands."

"Not if you didn't see me."

"There's no way in that I can't see you! Look, four of them TV's cover the other exits and I got this one. How the hell can I explain?"

"You won't have to."

"Oh boy, will I catch hell. No more tips for old Spud. It's gonna be real dry around here for a while. Maybe that long-haired relief kid will get my job."

"Don't worry," I said.

"So go ahead. Not even a monkey can get there anyway."

The elevator stopped at the top, the doors sliding open noiselessly. It was a bright blue foyer, decorated with modern sculpture and wildly colorful oil paintings in gold frames. The single door at the end was surrealistically decorated with a big eye painted around the peephole and I wondered how long ago it was that I was watched by another painted eye.

I touched the bell and waited. I touched it again, holding it in for a full minute, then let go and waited some more. I wasn't about to try to batter down three inches of oak, so I took out the .45 and blew each of the three locks out of their sockets. The noise of the shots was deafening in that confined space, but the door swung inward limply. I wasn't worried about the sound. It wasn't going to reach anyplace else. The tenants here were paying for absolute privacy that included soundproofing. Tomorrow the shattered door would even be an asset when the explanations started.

154

I walked through the rooms to the back of the building and into the bedroom that faced the fire escape, covered the catch with my sleeve, twisted it open, then raised the window the same way. All around me New York was staring, watching me with curious yellow eyes in the darker faces of the other buildings, seeing just one more thing to store away in memories that could never be tapped.

Gusts of wind whipped around the corner, driving the rain in angular sheets. I grinned again and started up the perforated steel steps to that other window and leaned against it with my shoulder, putting pressure to it gradually until the small pane cracked almost noiselessly. The pieces came out easily and I got my hand through the opening, undid the lock and shoved the window up. A swipe at the catch wiped out any prints and I was inside.

When I eased the door open I heard the subdued murmur of voices, the words indistinguishable. I was in a small office of some type, functional and modern, the kind a dedicated businessman whose work never stopped would have.

Maybe there would be things in there, I thought, *but let somebody else find it.*

I leaned on the ornate handle of the latch and tugged the door open.

The maid heard me, but never had time to see me. I laid a fast chop across her jaw as she turned around and she went down without a sound. I pulled her into the little office and closed the door on her. And I was in a dining area with the voices a little louder now because they were right behind the one more door I had to go through.

One of the voices smashed a hand on a table hard and in choked-up anger said, "How many times do I have to tell you? There was nothing! I looked everywhere!"

"It *had* to be there!" *I recognized that voice.*

"Don't tell me my job! It was *not* in the room. It was like all the other places. Maybe he did not have it at all. To him, what would it mean? Nothing, that's what. A single piece of paper with names of places written down. Why would he have kept that?"

Then there was another voice I recognized too, a cold, calm voice that could be jocular and friendly at other times. "He didn't have to know what it meant. It was something that came from the wallet of an important person who would keep only important things on that person. It would have a certain value. Why else would he have made those calls?" The voice paused a moment, then

155

added. "You know, it would have been easier to have paid his price."

The other one said, "A blackmailer could have photostated it. If it were valuable to me, it would have been equally as valuable to someone else."

"To whom would he sell?" the cold voice asked.

"Who knows how a mind like his would work? Perhaps a newspaperman, or by now he might have even suspected just what he did hold. You realize what it would be worth then, the price he could demand for it? That's all it would take to smash everything we have built. We couldn't take the chance."

"I'm afraid the chance has already been taken," the flat voice stated. "Now there is no time for any alternative. We simply have to wait. At this point there is little possibility that we will fail. If the document is hidden or destroyed, it will stay hidden or destroyed. There is not enough time left for anyone to pursue the matter further. I suggest you ring for that maid again and inquire about our drinks so we can conclude this affair."

From another room I heard the annoyed sound of a buzzer. It rang again, then a voice I knew so well said, "Stanley, go see what's keeping her."

I stepped away from the door and crowded behind the angle of an ornate china closet. The door opened and clicked shut on its own closing device and I saw the face of the man who had come in, a still angry face at having been chewed out for bungling the job. It wasn't a new face. I had seen it twice before this night, once in a burst of gunfire at the top of the stairs and again coming out of an elevator in the hotel where Beaver had been sliced to death like Lippy Sullivan.

Like Lippy Sullivan.

The man called Stanley crossed the room and pushed open the swinging door that led into the kitchen calling loudly for somebody named Louise. He never heard me follow him in, but when he didn't find Louise he spun around and I let him see me, one big surprised look, and he knew who I was and why I was there and before he could get the knife out of his belt with an incredibly fast snatch and thrust, I leaned aside and threw a fist into his face that sent his features into a crazy caricature of a human and left teeth imbedded in my knuckles and a sudden spurt of blood spraying both of us.

I should have shot him and had it over with, but I didn't want it to happen that fast. I was a pig and wanted him all for myself and slowly and almost made a mistake.

He was a pro and strong. He was hurt and death could be the next step and he was moving and thinking even before he hit the floor. He didn't waste breath yelling. What strength he had left kept the knife in his hand, his feet scrabbling for survival.

The blade flashed around when I jumped him, the gun forgotten now. All I wanted was to use my hands. I got my fingers in his hair and yanked his head around, pounding my fist against his ear. I saw the knife come up and blocked it with my knee, the razor edge slicing into my skin, then I let go of his hair and grabbed his wrist.

He was strong, but I had gotten to him first and he wasn't that strong any more. He was flat out under me and I was bringing his own knife up under his throat and this time he knew it couldn't be stopped and he tried to let out the yell he had held in. Then my knee caught him square in the balls with such impact he almost died then, eyes bugging out of his head in sheer agony.

He still fought, and he was still able to see what was happening when his own hand drove the knife completely through his neck until it was imbedded in the floor behind.

I picked up my rod and eased the hammer back.

Okay, Lippy, it was almost paid for.

You shouldn't stop and think back. I should have known that. All the years in the business and I forgot a little thing that could kill you. It wasn't instinct that turned me in time. It was accident. I should have known they'd send another one out to see what had happened and he was standing there behind me with a gun coming out of his pocket, a flat, ugly little thing with a deadly snout ready to spit.

But you don't beat a guy to the draw who already has a gun in his fist, and I triggered the .45 into a roaring blast that caught him just off center from his nose and threw the entire back of his skull against the door. I was over him before he had crumpled to the tiles and met the other one coming in and this time I was ready. He only saw me as the slug was tearing his chest apart, dropped the Luger and stood there in momentary surprise, then fell in a lifeless heap, blocking the doorway.

Chairs crashed backward outside and there was a shrill scream cutting through the curses. I kicked the corpse out of the way, yanked the door open in time to see that smiling, pleasant Mr. Kudak who was so political, who had come from one regime into another without anybody ever knowing about it, picking himself up off the floor. He didn't have a gun, but he had a mind that was even more

157

dangerous so I blew it right out of its braincase without the slightest compunction and ran across the room, jumping the knocked-over furniture, and reached the door just as it was locked in my face.

They shouldn't have bothered. One shot took the lock away and I kicked the door open and stood there with the .45 aimed at William Dorn who was pulling a snub-nosed revolver from the desk drawer, then swung the .45 to cover Renée Talmage who was standing there beside him. They never saw me thumb the empty .45 back into the loaded position.

"Don't bother, William," I said. "Toss it in the middle of the floor."

For a second I thought he'd try for me anyway and I got that strange feeling up across my shoulders. *I knew what would happen if he did.* But there are those who can plan violence and those who could execute it. He wasn't one of those who could pull the trigger.

Right now he was thinking and I knew that too. I could take them in, say what I had to say, and while the police held them the big death would be released and all he had to do was wait long enough and everybody would be gone except them and they could walk out easily enough.

I grinned and said, "It couldn't happen that way, William."

They looked at each other. Finally he straightened and tried to regain his composure. "What?"

"You could be in a cell. So everybody's dead. You'd still be in a cell and you'd starve to death anyway."

Renée spoke for the first time. "Mike . . ."

"Shut up, Renée. For a whole lifetime I'm going to have to look back and remember that I liked you once. It's going to be a damn nasty memory as it is, so for now, just shut up."

Now there was something about the way they looked at each other. And I was enjoying myself. It was going to be fun bringing them in like this. They'd hate me so hard after it they would never be able to live with themselves.

"You never should have killed the wrong man, William," I said. "Just think, if your bright boys had really been on the ball when they went after that pickpocket and found where he was living, you would have won the whole ball game. But no, they put the knife to the wrong boy, and the right one hit the road. He was a sharp article too and when he knew what was chasing him he pulled out all the stops. Right then he knew what he had was important and started playing his own game."

158

"See here . . ."

"Knock it off. It's over, William. The trouble with Beaver was, he didn't know who really was out to kill him. The only stuff worth while was what he had from you and Woody Ballinger. He tried to tap you both and almost got tapped out by Woody first. Old Woody has manpower too.

"I guess you thought I was a real clown getting into the act, stumbling all over trying to square things with a nobody who had gotten himself knocked off. Brother, you should have done your homework better. I work on the dark side of the fence myself."

Renée was watching me, her hands clasping and unclasping, something desperate in her eyes. "You're a cutie, honey," I told her. "The act in your apartment was neat, real neat. You saw those pictures I had of Beaver and slipped one out of my pocket when I was lying there all nice and naked and getting beautifully vibrated. You slipped it to your maid to deliver to William here when she was supposed to go to the drugstore. It doesn't take a half hour to go to a drugstore a block away. Then all the manpower went into high gear again. I went and laid out the story for you in detail that made things nice and easy. You got bullet-creased by an enemy I was on to so I thought you were square with me . . . not the real enemy after all. I'm getting old, chums. I'm just not thinking hard enough, I guess. In my own way I have a little luck here and there, and people make mistakes. Like William's maid mentioning the meeting here tonight and you not being sharp enough to have your maid tell me you were sleeping in case I called.

"Maybe all the excitement was too much for you. Things were coming to a head and you were ready to be king and queen. Now I'm going to tell you something. You never would have made it. That vaccine doesn't make you immune."

This time their eyes met, held a second, and the fear was there all the way.

I said, "We know the story, at least most of it. Now there will be time to dig the rest of it out. Nobody will ever know about it though and that's the way it should be. Maybe now some of this crappy rivalry between countries will slow down and there will be some sensible cooperation. I doubt it, but it may happen for a while and even that's better than nothing. I found your little sheet of onionskin, William, all nicely detailing where those cannisters were planted and right now every one of them is being located and deactivated. If you don't believe me I'll name a few."

I gave him four and he knew for certain then.

"By tomorrow there will be some other things added. It won't take the pros long to get all the names of your people and the net will tighten quickly and tightly and all your beautiful hopes will go up in smoke."

Something about them had changed. It had started when they looked at each other. It had grown fast, and now they looked at each other again, a resigned look that had a peculiar meaning to it and William Dorn said, "We go nowhere, Mr. Hammer."

"You're going with me," I told him. "Consider yourself lucky. At least here you get due process of law. Your own people would kill you the slowest way they know how."

"They would manage somehow anyway, I'm afraid."

"That's your tough luck," I said.

"No, long ago we prepared for such an eventuality. The preparation was drastic and simply an eventuality, but the time has come and now there can be no other way. We both have been fitted with cyanide capsules, Mr. Hammer. I'm sorry to spoil your fun."

Once more, they looked at each other, both nodding almost imperceptibly, and there was a minute movement of the lines of their jaws.

I could see the death coming on, but they sure as hell weren't going to spoil my fun.

"Too bad," I said. "You still had another way out." I looked at the stubby revolver that was lying on the floor near their feet and very slowly I raised the .45 to my own temple. I pulled the trigger and there was only that flat, metallic click of the hammer snapping shut on nothing.

They both tried to scream a protest at the world and lunged for the gun on the floor at the same time. They could take me with them ... the final pleasure would be theirs after all.

Renée had the gun in her fingers and William Dorn was trying to tear it from her when the cyanide hit them with one final spasm.

And I was laughing in a very quiet room.